Introduct

I first encountered Howard Tayler at a local science fiction convention. I saw his name on the program listing and thought to myself "A local webcomic artist? Why haven't I heard of this before?" Now, I'm something of a webcomics junkie, and considered myself well-versed in the landscape. I was surprised I hadn't heard of this Tayler guy, and assumed that he was probably an aspiring artist with an amateur comic.

Boy, was I wrong.

Howard is good at this; very good. I can say this with authority, as the comic had a difficult challenge to surmount in converting me. When I returned from that convention, I sat down to read the archives, but was already predisposed to find fault. I assumed that the comic would be second rate, and when I hit the first few strips--which even Howard will tell you have some pretty rough art--I seemingly found confirmation of my expectations. But, as always, I was willing to give the archives a little bit of reading before giving up on the comic.

I was surprised at what I found. Yes, the art was bad. But the writing was surprisingly sharp and the jokes were good--some of them were even great. I continued to read on, and I discovered what you will discover if you read this collection: A webcomic written and drawn by a man who not only understands how to be funny, but who also understands how to tell a great science fiction story.

I was so impressed that I read through the entire archives, already years long by that point. The art got better, the jokes got more consistent, and most importantly for me, the storytelling got deep. It's tough to find a comic which can balance all of those different elements, and it's even tougher to find a comic which can continue to keep that balance going over years of storytelling.

In my opinion, *The Teraport Wars* is where *Schlock Mercenary* really starts to figure out what it wants to be when it grows up. By this point the art has come a long way, and the storytelling hits its stride. You'll find quick pacing mixed with deep worldbuilding, both of which are strong enough to hold up against any published science fiction novel. This is the book where Howard shows that he can make the cultures, politics, and characters of his world more than just window-dressing for his jokes.

But, fortunately, those jokes don't go away. In fact, I think that the strength of characterization and setting only helps them improve. Howard has the rare ability to make us laugh without casting us out of his story; we can enjoy the jokes while at the same time feeling tension when the characters are in danger. That's something that even Douglas Adams, for all of his wit, could never do for me.

So, sit back, grab a mug of your favorite warmed beverage, and enjoy. You're in for a treat.

Brandon Sanderson

May 5, 2008

QUEST FOR SECOND SIGHT PART I: THROUGH THE AGES

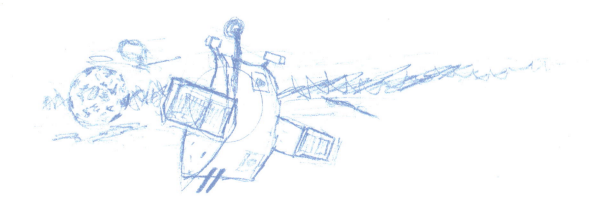

THE TERAPORT WARS

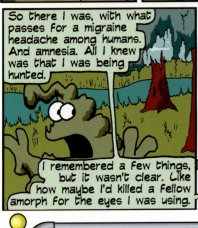

Note: The full story of Schlock's circus adventures can be found in *Schlock Mercenary: Under New Management* and *Schlock Mercenary: The Blackness Between*.

Quest For Second Sight Part I: Through The Ages

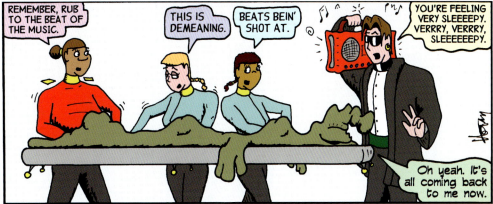

The Teraport Wars

Quest for Second Sight Part I: Through the Ages

Note: For those interested in the relevant details, Schlock was able (under hypnosis) to clearly describe the rescue vessel that pulled him from the holed pirate craft he was aboard. That description pegged the ship as belonging to the government of the *Bhaan-triit*, whose enforcement logs could then be searched for records of the event. This led to the discovery of the registry (forged, but still trackable) of the pirate craft, which was tracked back two jumps to the *Uuna-Uuna-g'Thwap* system. No prior jump was recorded, but that system's wormgate is a serial gate rather than a hub gate, and is only tuned for "upstream" and "downstream" travel, which narrowed the search for the source of the original jump to two possible systems in the serial gate sequence. The upstream (away from the galactic core) system, *Parhchintofleekybok*, was one the pirate craft must have traveled through to get to *Uuna-Uuna-g'Thwap*, since its gate was also serial, and *Parhchintofleekybok* was too heavily developed to match Schlock's story. Thus, three jumps in from the hub system of *Bhaan-triit*, Petey identified *Ghanj-Rho* as Schlock's point of origin.

So now you know. Aren't you glad you asked?

Aritst Commentary:

Uniocs are a fun race to draw because they are so inherently funny. Who wouldn't laugh at the one big eye and two hovering eyebrows? When I needed pirates for the Quest for Second Sight storyline, I picked uniocs because putting an eye patch on one is hilarious.

unioc pirate

Schlock Mercenary

Quest For Second Sight Part I: Through the Ages

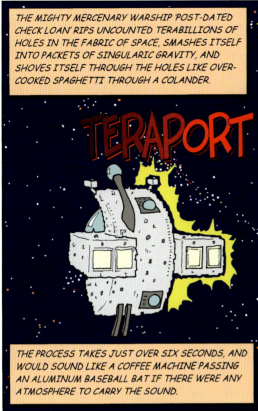

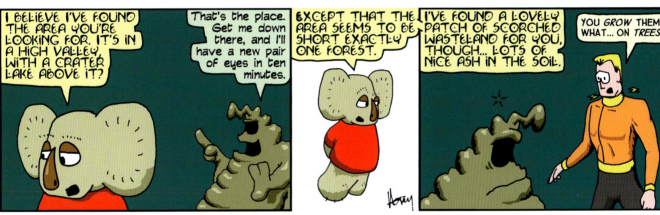

Quest for Second Sight Part I: Through the Ages

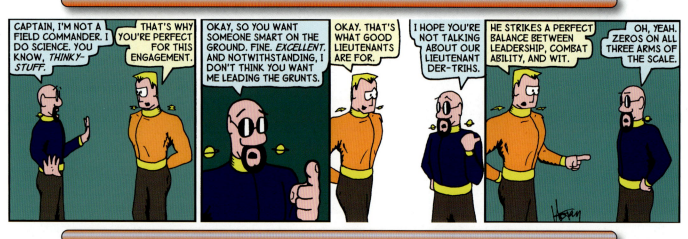
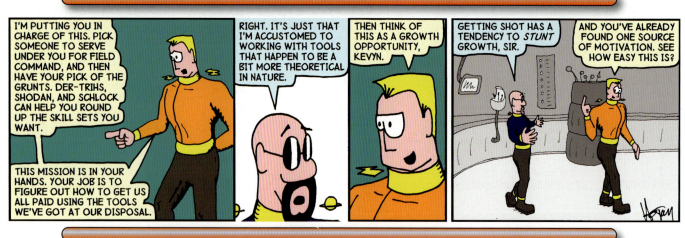

Quest For Second Sight Part I: Through the Ages

Note: It may surprise some readers to learn how well-read Captain Tagon is. After all, while some images may be part of the collective 'common knowledge,' not everybody knows what a koala looks like.

Artist commentary:

I don't like working with colored pencils. The result always looks like crayon, only without the childlike innocence of crayon work. This probably means I'm doing it wrong, and is just one of the reasons the comic is colored digitally.

The Teraport Wars

Quest for Second Sight Part I: Through the Ages

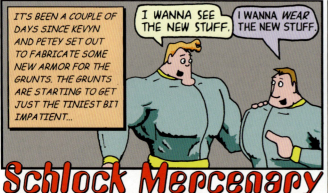

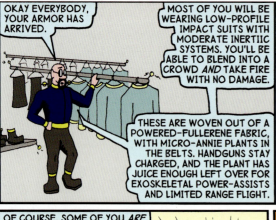
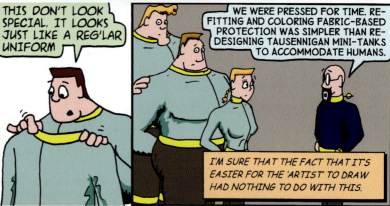

Note: The Tausennigan mini-tanks Petey has blueprints for are made for Tausennigan Ob'enn soldiers, most of whom are between 1 and 1.5 meters tall. Elf is only about 4 centimeters taller than that, and she's slender, so the only thing that needed re-working in the design was some of the interfaces. The 'tanks can double as dog-fighters, providing both air-cover and ground support. They are moderately stealthy (when parked... there's nothing stealthy about a full-sphere grav shield) and can dump waste heat with 99.99% efficiency through the weapons systems. Armed with energy weapons, mass-slingers, and a solid supply of smart munitions, these things can kick unholy quantities of ponderous butt. They just can't carry pilots with ponderous butts.

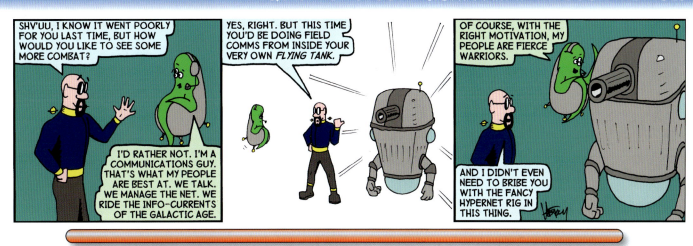

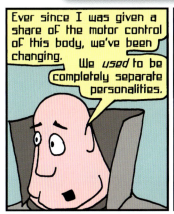

Quest for Second Sight Part I: Through the Ages

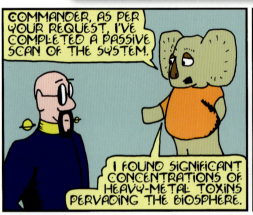

Note: A hematic scrubber processes blood at the gastrointestinal interfaces and passes the neutrally-wrapped toxins into the fecal system for disposal. Half the point of a hematic scrubber is to keep you healthy. The other half of the point is to remind you that you should not put down roots here. This is accomplished by discouraging the patient from sitting for an extended period.

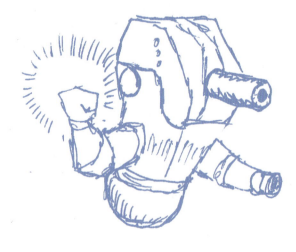

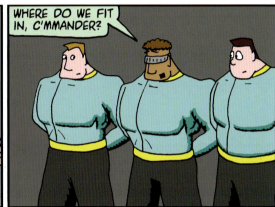
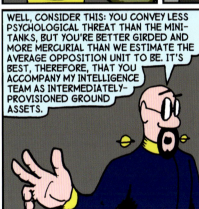

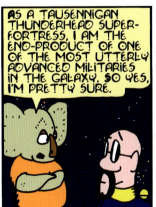

Quest for Second Sight Part I: Through the Ages

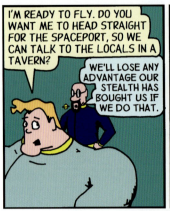
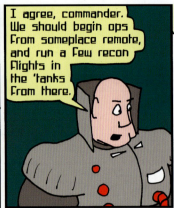

> Note: One may wonder what uses are found for gasoline, a messy source of chemical energy, in an economy where far more advanced power sources are widely available.
>
> Contextually, it would appear to have at least anecdotal use in relation to cats.

Schlock Mercenary

Quest For Second Sight Part I: Through The Ages

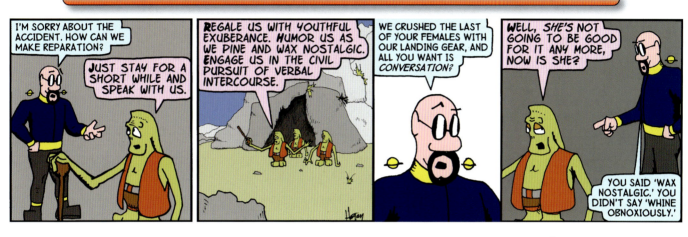

Artist commentary:

When I designed the Bradicor I was shooting for "wrinkly," "old," and "short," but I didn't want them to look like Yoda. This was solved by leaving off their ears. Also, I'm not sure the tail in this sketch ever made it to the final design. It's possible that it falls off with extreme old age.

stone hut

The Teraport Wars

QUEST FOR SECOND SIGHT PART I: THROUGH THE AGES

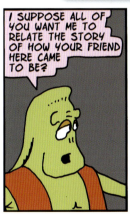

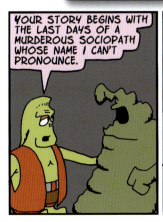

Quest for Second Sight Part I: Through the Ages

Artist commentary:

Every so often authors have these "ah-HAH!" moments. Discovering that amorphs do battle with secreted chemical weapons was that kind of moment for me. It made a lot more sense than two creatures simply ripping pieces off of each other and trying to throw the bits farther away than the other guy did.

Quest For Second Sight Part I: Through The Ages

Quest for Second Sight Part I: Through the Ages

Note: Since the epidemic of earthlings burst upon Galactic Culture in the late 21st century (Human Pre-diaspora Calendar), societies across the breadth and depth of the spiral ancient humans quaintly called the 'Milky Way' have been infected with choice bits of human language, culture, and even religion.

Christmas, unfortunately, stopped being a religious event long, long before the first unioc smuggler celebrated it. Those few religious purists remaining among the humans might claim that galactic culture corrupted the holiday, but most 31st century historians are confident that the fault can be squarely placed on the television producers responsible for 'Rudolph the Red-Nosed Reindeer.'

In most Galactic languages, the expression "Merry Christmas" differs in meaning from the phrase "Look at what I bought for you" in only one way. Idiomatically, it means "Look at what I bought for you" with the unspoken-but-fully-expressed sentiment "No, you may not have the receipt."

Ghanj-Rho, Tobir Spaceport

Quest For Second Sight Part I: Through The Ages

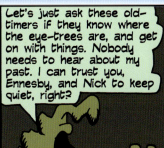

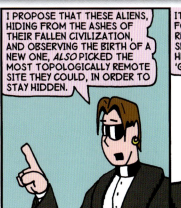

The Teraport Wars

Quest for Second Sight Part I: Through the Ages

QUEST FOR SECOND SIGHT PART II: THROUGH A DARKENED GLASS

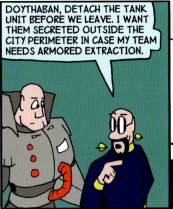

> Note: For those of you who have not read Schlock Mercenary from the beginning, Kevyn is making reference to the time Schlock poured beer on his plasgun with catastrophic results.
>
> The last tavern we visited in the strip suffered minor damage, and required some paint. Anyone who cares to wager that the next tavern will get off with just paint is likely to lose money faster than a venture capitalist in a dot-com gold rush.

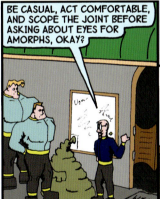

THE TERAPORT WARS

Quest for Second Sight Part II: Through a Darkened Glass

Quest for Second Sight Part II: Through a Darkened Glass

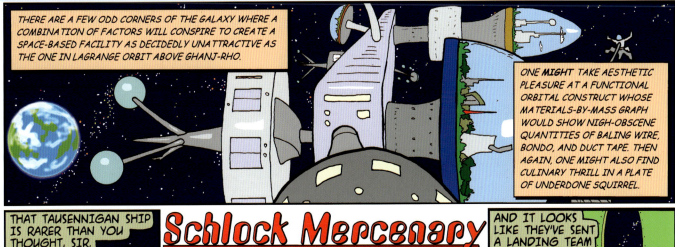

There are a few odd corners of the galaxy where a combination of factors will conspire to create a space-based facility as decidedly unattractive as the one in Lagrange orbit above Ghanj-Rho.

One MIGHT take aesthetic pleasure at a functional orbital construct whose materials-by-mass graph would show nigh-obscene quantities of baling wire, bondo, and duct tape. Then again, one might also find culinary thrill in a plate of underdone squirrel.

Schlock Mercenary

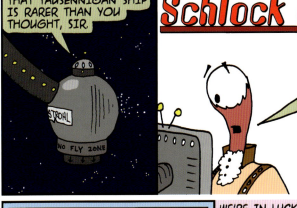

That Tausennigan ship is rarer than you thought, sir.

Sure, there are only eight other ships like it outside of the psycho-bear military. But if the registry match I've got is accurate, this one has also been retrofitted with those new teraport drives, and probably has a few weapons and defenses based on the same technology.

And it looks like they've sent a landing team down to Jun-Cho's.

Pick 'em up. If we want that ship, we can start by taking a few hostages.

And so the local enforcers are dispatched, flying their skymounts with air-tearing haste.

After all, it's best that the welcoming committee not be late to greet guests.

We're in luck, dispatch says that Jun-Cho has them corralled in his bar.

Maybe not... isn't that Jun-Cho's bouncer?

WHUMP

It is. And it's unfortunate for him that he does not bounce better.

Note: The 21st century jury-rigger will no doubt be familiar with baling wire, bondo, and duct tape. By the 31st century, these materials have evolved significantly, but are still recognizable.

Baling wire, for instance, has largely been overshadowed by malleable carbonan/polymer superfilaments, which are at least ten times stronger and 100 times more expensive. For this reason, many 31st-century jury-riggers will choose the economical route and just use five times as much baling wire. The trick is finding it (there's a spool of it in the garage, underneath the hedge laser).

Bondo has seen many evolutionary iterations, the most popular being a nanomotile goop (brand name, 'NuBondo') that sets when you send the appropriate command to the nanobots. The 'bots are re-useable as long as you can keep them fed with the right nutrient solution. Unfortunately, by the time you realize you need the stuff you'll find that the kids have dumped all the 'bots in the aquarium for a 1/100,000,000th scale recreation of the Europan Rebellion, much to the dismay of the fish. You'll end up resorting to regular old Bondo, provided you've remembered to put the lid on it.

Duct Tape has actually seen the most change during the intervening centuries. For instance, it can now safely be used to fasten and seal duct-work. Just be sure to lose the handy-dandy spool with the built-in tape cutter before it trims the tape just above your first knuckle.

The Teraport Wars

Quest for Second Sight Part II: Through a Darkened Glass

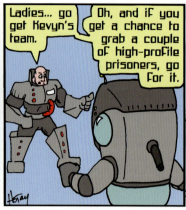

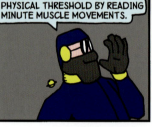

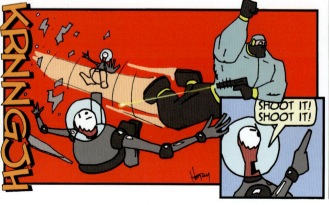

QUEST FOR SECOND SIGHT PART II: THROUGH A DARKENED GLASS

Artist commentary:

I've always been fascinated by the relative sizes of people. This may stem from the fact that I'm rather small of stature myself, but frequent the gym where people of much larger stature may be found. This particular sketch was an effort to juxtapose Elf's diminuitive five-foot-two-inch height with Brad, who is seven feet tall. Of course then I had to stick somebody in the middle, so I picked Nick, who is a little over six-foot-three.

THE TERAPORT WARS

Quest for Second Sight Part II: Through a Darkened Glass

Schlock Mercenary

QUEST FOR SECOND SIGHT PART II: THROUGH A DARKENED GLASS

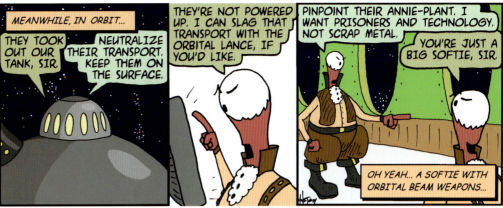

Note: The discriminating reader of science fiction will be well aware of the fact that many beam weapons available in the 21st century suffer from a small dispersal problem over long ranges. Specifically, from the L5 orbit provided by Ghanj-Rho's natural satellite, a simple laser could have a beam width comparable to that of a football field (assuming that the football field was a beam, which pretty well rules out any definition of the word 'football' that you care to use).

Bear in mind, though, that we are talking about 31st-century beam weapons. The orbital lance in use by the Gamm faction in today's strip does not suffer from appreciable dispersal problems, thanks in part to an extended gravitic tunnel that shapes the particle beam while imparting near-cee velocity to the particles fired.

The non-discriminating reader of science fiction should look at today's strip and say "whoa... cool. I gotta get me some of that."

THE TERAPORT WARS

Quest for Second Sight Part II: Through a Darkened Glass

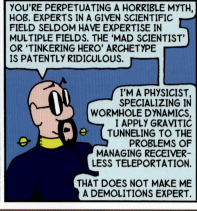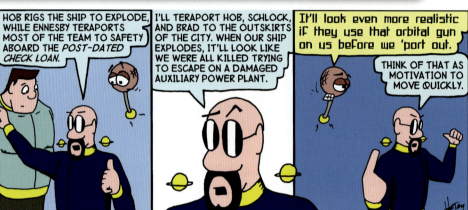

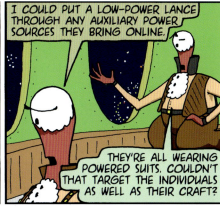

Note: Many of you may be considering asking why the Metisoid in the third panel has two heads. Whatever you do, don't ask *her*. It would not be polite, and she's already in a bad mood.

Quest for Second Sight Part II: Through a Darkened Glass

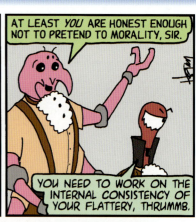

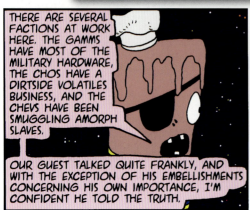

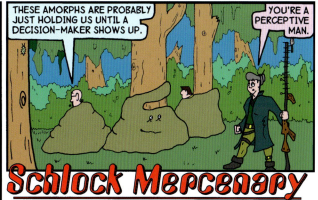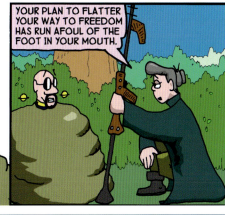

Quest for Second Sight Part II: Through a Darkened Glass

Artist commentary:

When I sat down to visually design the Emily Veldtfontweg character (note: her last name can be roughly translated as "springfield") I didn't do an especially good job of differentiating her from the Admiral Breya character. Lots of readers emailed me or posted in the forums to ask if the two were somehow related. They're not, but I never could deny that they look a lot alike.

I suppose it's safe for me to confess now that the accidental similarity gave me some ideas for how the story would wrap up.

Quest for Second Sight Part II: Through a Darkened Glass

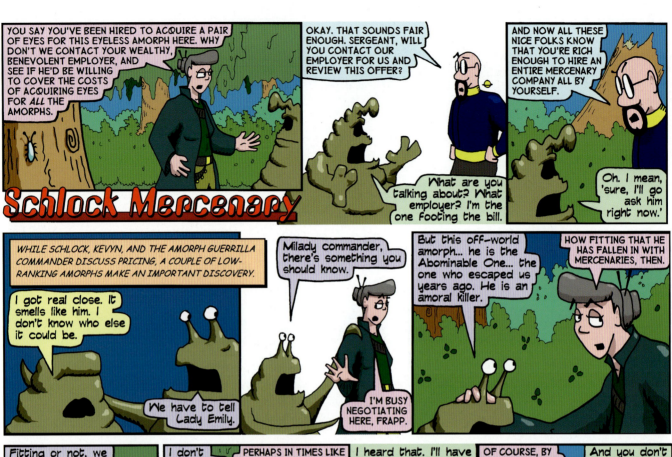

QUEST FOR SECOND SIGHT PART II: THROUGH A DARKENED GLASS

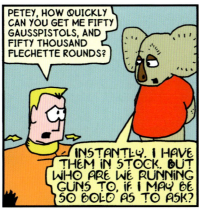

Note: Any grade-school student should be able to tell you that at a continuous rate of fire, fifty gauss-pistols would need to fire 8.3333[repeating] rounds per second in order to go through 50,000 rounds in two minutes. What a grade school student might not be able to tell you is that 8 rounds a second is sloooow.

Unrelated Note: Some readers may be alarmed to see how willing Tagon is to culturally contaminate aboriginal aliens in order to achieve a military objective. Addressing those concerns, the author has this response:

It makes for a good science-fiction adventure to have the captain say something along the lines of "prime directive be damned." It makes for much better science-fiction, however, to have the captain able to say in frank honesty "I have no idea what this prime directive concept is, and it sounds like foolishness that belongs in another universe entirely. Go away. I have work to do." If you persisted in whining about native cultures, that captain would have no choice but to shoot you.

THE TERAPORT WARS

37

Quest for Second Sight Part II: Through a Darkened Glass

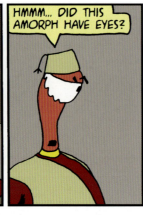

Note: The Hypernet Biblioversity Library Dictionary, 234th ed., defines "maimery" as follows:

Maimery: n. Mayhem, conflagration, conflict, or applied force resulting in the loss of one or more limbs.

It should not be confused with *mammary*. The two words have nothing to do with each other and have only appeared in adjacent context in those few publications low-brow enough to cover the Hefner Heir Wars of 2116 (and in this footnote, but that doesn't count.)

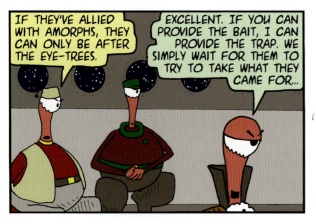

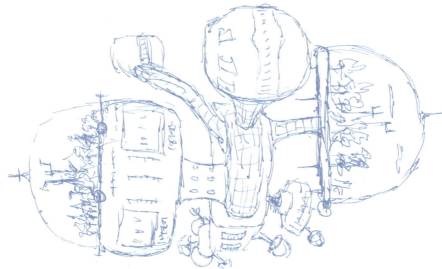

Quest for Second Sight Part III: Through the Roof

Schlock Mercenary

The Teraport Wars

Quest for Second Sight Part III: Through the Roof

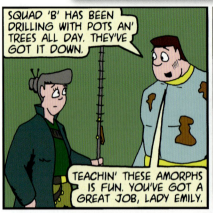

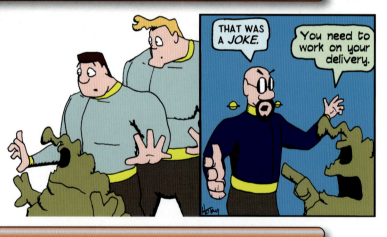

Quest for Second Sight Part III: Through the Roof

Note: For those of you wondering how Commander Gamm knows how many crew Tagon has, keep in mind that at one point Tagon's Toughs was publicly traded, and as such had to maintain a public crew manifest.

Another Note: Oh, and for those of you who are not versed in Unioc mythology, the eye-fairy is a blind hag who sneaks into the bedchambers of those who bear false witness, and plucks off their eye. Then she leaves them a nice, shiny coin. This story is used by Unioc parents to encourage honesty among their children. Naturally, their children delight in these tales of night-time violence and grow up to be honest, well-adjusted adults (who knowingly relate the fib to THEIR children, flying blind in the face of irony) ... another example of the fruits of solid parenting practices.

The vomit demon is a tale conjured up by the parents of fussy eaters and, without going into much detail about Unioc gastronomy, let's just say that it works for Unioc children. It most certainly would NOT work on me.

The Teraport Wars

Quest for Second Sight Part III: Through the Roof

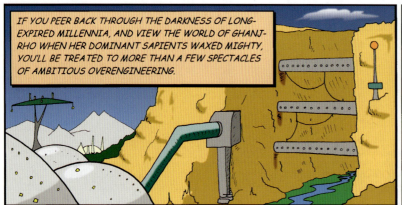

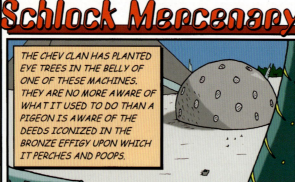
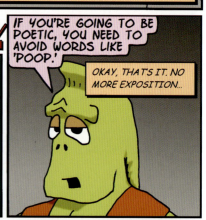

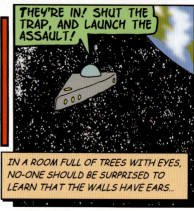

Quest for Second Sight Part III: Through the Roof

Note: Those readers familiar with the early 21st-century coastline of Florida may be concerned at the inaccuracy in the rendering of that fine isthmus in today's strip. (Yes, I said "isthmus" instead of "peninsula"). Suffice it to say that with the global warming and resulting superhurricanes of the late 21st century (not to mention Mother Nature's pendulum-effect and follow up ice-age in the early 22nd) the coastline changed a bit. And those are just the naturally induced changes. We won't go into the creation of Lake Yucatan by King Louis Castro XIV.

Artist commentary:

I'm not sure what these two are arguing about. I'd like to imagine that Kevyn is right, but that seems to happen a lot.

The Teraport Wars

43

Quest for Second Sight Part III: Through the Roof

Quest for Second Sight Part III: Through the Roof

Note: Ornithologists might be hard-pressed to positively classify any of Ghanj-Rho's harblewheezers (the common harblewheezer, duffle-downy harblewheezer, eastern harblewheezer, puck-freckled harblewheezer, or the elusive slandy-juicing harblewheezer) as 'birds,' per se, given their complete lack of that peculiar cellular buckling structure that gives rise to proper feathers. Even the duffle-downy harblewheezer is not so much 'downy' as it is 'hairy.' Still, as far as most of the rest of us are concerned, they lay eggs, fly, and defecate whilst airborne, so birds they must be.

Harblewheezer eggs have a curious protein lining inside the shell that serves to make the harblewheezer hatchling quite smelly and offensive to the taste of even the most indiscriminating of Ghanj-Rho's omnivores (that means amorphs). Thus, having a broken harblewheezer egg in your mouth would lead you to hurl pretty much involuntarily (assuming you were an amorph, which some readers have expressed a wish to be [and this phenomenon continues to baffle the sociology staff here at Schlock Mercenary]). Yuck.

It's interesting to note that the names for the various (we'll go ahead and call them) birds of Ghanj-Rho have the same sort of absurd, 'did-you-sound-that-out-before-writing-it-down' naming as birds elsewhere in the galaxy (hairy woodpecker, or tufted titmouse, anyone?). This is easily explained. The sort of people who go out of their way to spot birds and draw pictures of them in fieldbooks are just plain bent.

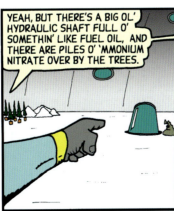

THE TERAPORT WARS

Quest for Second Sight Part III: Through the Roof

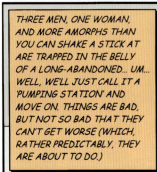
THREE MEN, ONE WOMAN, AND MORE AMORPHS THAN YOU CAN SHAKE A STICK AT ARE TRAPPED IN THE BELLY OF A LONG-ABANDONED... UM... WELL, WE'LL JUST CALL IT A 'PUMPING STATION' AND MOVE ON. THINGS ARE BAD, BUT NOT SO BAD THAT THEY CAN'T GET WORSE (WHICH, RATHER PREDICTABLY, THEY ARE ABOUT TO DO.)

KEVYN, I'M READY TA BLAST US OUTTA HERE. JUST SAY THE WORD, AN' I'LL TELL MISTER PRIMER DOWN IN THE HOLE TA DO HIS LITTLE DANCE.

NOT YET, HOB. I NEED TO MAKE SURE IT'S CLEAR OUTSIDE. I'M GOING TO BREAK SILENCE AND CALL IN OUR AIR SUPPORT.

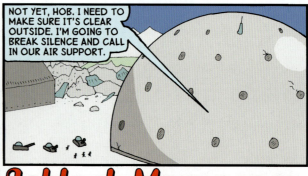

Schlock Mercenary

PETEY, WE'VE GOT A PROBLEM DOWN HERE. WE NEED EXTRACTION, AND I DON'T THINK YOU CAN TERAPORT THE MINI-TANKS ALL THE WAY IN.

MINI-TANKS WON'T HELP KEVYN. SCANS SHOW THAT THEY'VE PULLED IN SOME HEAVY ARMOR OUTSIDE.

THEN THEY MUST HAVE LAID A TRAP FOR US, AND WE WALKED RIGHT INTO IT. PETEY, WE NEED FULL AIR SUPPORT. YOU'D BETTER PLOW ON DOWN HERE YOURSELF AND GET US OUT.

IT'S NOT THAT SIMPLE. THEY'VE LAID A TRAP FOR ME, TOO.

A VERITABLE ARMADA OF LIGHT CRAFT HAS SURROUNDED ME, AND IS PRESSING ME WITH THAT ORBITAL LANCE.

I CAN EXTRACT YOU, BUT I HAVE TO SWAT THESE FLIES FIRST.

YOU'RE A BIG, MEAN WARSHIP. THAT SHOULDN'T TAKE LONG, RIGHT?

UNDER ORDINARY CIRCUMSTANCES, NO, IT SHOULD NOT TAKE LONG.

THIS IS THE PART WHERE THINGS GET WORSE...

THEY ARE DEMANDING THAT I ALLOW MYSELF TO BE BOARDED.

IF I RESIST, THEY CLAIM THAT THEY WILL KILL ALL OF YOU... STARTING WITH THE AMORPHS.

WHATEVER YOU DO, DON'T GO THINKING THAT THINGS CAN ONLY GET BETTER FROM HERE.

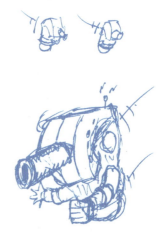

Quest for Second Sight Part III: Through the Roof

NOTE: Let's play a game of Superfortress Space Siege, shall we?

You Will Need: ONE (1) Tausennigan Ob'enn Thunderhead Superfortress, and an ARMADA (lots'n'lots) of smaller ships. All ships should have equally modern weapons and shielding, but the superfortress gets more of both.

To Play: The Superfortress starts out surrounded by the armada of smaller vessels. The cards are dealt by the Three Fates, Lady Luck, or your choice of destiny-deity. Play proceeds counter-clockwise to the dealer's left (which of course means that the players are upside-down in relation to the dealer. This is okay).

Strategy for the armada: Force the fortress to raise gravitic shielding by pressing it from all sides with heavy beam weapons. Clear away any hypernet drones it may have left outside its shield, thus leaving it blind to frequencies blocked by the shield (and if you've got a broad-spectrum of beam weapons on it, the shield will be quite opaque.) Then move in with a coordinated assault of small torpedoes with gravitic breachers.

Strategy for the Superfortress: Push your shield out as far as you can, while still retaining enough power to swat incoming torpedoes. Hope you get them all before they get too close. Push shielded drones through your shields so you can see. Push shielded, guided torpedoes through your shields in hopes of keeping the armada on its proverbial toes. Fly around half-blind, forcing individual armada ships into range of your gravitic weapons (your gravy-gun range is longer than theirs is).

The game ends when the armada runs out of torpedoes, or when the superfortress drops its shields. The winner is the player who can walk away from the game under his own power and find something safer to do.

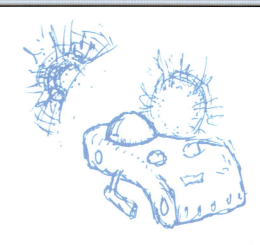

Quest for Second Sight Part III: Through the Roof

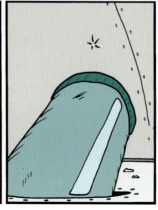

Quest for Second Sight Part III: Through the Roof

Schlock Mercenary presents Famous Last Words

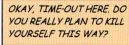

The Teraport Wars

Quest for Second Sight Part III: Through the Roof

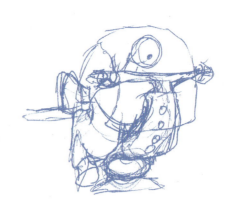

Elf takes prisoners

Elf, Chelle, and Shv'uu have a dirty job to do.
We gotta draw off those tanks, but we can't take 'em in a fair fight.

I've got a map of the Cho, Chev, and Gamm interests down here in the city. We have to hit undefended targets.
Oh, no... what about innocent civilians?

Doythaban tells me that they're all guilty of something...
But I'm telling you that I want to be able to sleep tonight.

So I found us a big, expensive, fully automated refinery to blow up.
It's the ultimate low-calorie hit — twice the blam, and not a shred of that pesky remorse.

Petey, we're gonna blow the dome down here. No more stalling. Just get here as fast as you can.

Roger that, Commander. I'm moving already.

Captain, shall I give the armada notice? You know, the standard clear out or be destroyed?
Sure. But don't use standard hailing protocols.

What protocol did you have in mind, sir?
Oh, I don't know. Let's just say that actions speak louder than words.

In order for the reader to understand the tactical situation, it is necessary to employ an analogy.

Commander Gamm thinks his little armada is attacking an under-staffed warship... one without a proper A.I. to coordinate the many weapon systems. Picture a man with a stack of flyswatters fending off a swarm of bees.

Gamm is rather fatally mistaken. His armada is up against a state of the art A.I, one capable of driving every single weapon aboard the superfortress with full efficiency, and to maximum effect.

This is the point at which the analogy falls apart...

AAAIIEEE... IT BURNS!

SCHLOCK MERCENARY

Quest for Second Sight Part III: Through the Roof

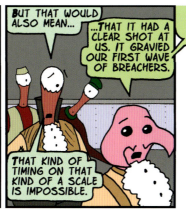

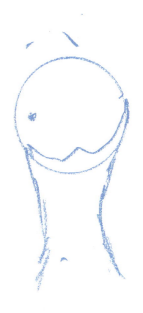

Note: Commander Gamm has three seconds on his hands (he may actually have more, but right now those three seconds are all he has confidence in). You might think that he wastes the first second on an expression of surprise and shock, but you'd be overlooking the intense metabolic activity during that period. His blood pressure leaps up, forcing more oxygen through the semipermeable membranes of his brain cells, (for those of you who are wondering, Gamm's brain sits in his pelvic cradle, about fifteen centimeters below his heart, and just four centimeters above the lower end of his digestive tract) and large quantities of endorphine-analogues are released into his system. Were he being attacked by a togrun (think "scaly tiger"), he'd be in prime condition to leap, kick, throw a spear, climb a tree, and then die screaming.

In the second second (not the same as second^2) Gamm quickly discards the primal urges of leaping, kicking, or tree climbing, spins to make eye-contact with the terapedo (okay, okay... the 'pedo has no eyes, per se), and feels the familiar, sickening push of a gravitic shield, telling him that this device is not going to fall prey to a sidearm.

Before the third second begins, Gamm's life starts to flash backwards before his eye. His consciousness expands, consuming the bounteous metabolic resources at its disposal, and for a one-point-four second eternity he is able to analyze everything he has ever said or done. In particular he considers the rather poor decision to have minions of his steal a Strohl T.A.D. III system (Teraport Area Denial Mark Three) from a passing sales rep, rather than simply buying a whole case of the stupid things.

The Teraport Wars

Quest for Second Sight Part III: Through the Roof

SOME INTERESTING EXPLOSIONS, MERE SECONDS APART...

THE CHO REFINERY BLAZES MERRILY.

THE CHEV DOME SPLITS BEHIND HOB'S SACRIFICIAL PIPE-BOMB.

THE GAMM FLAGSHIP BURSTS UNDER DIRECT TERAPEDO HIT.

AND THE LIBERATION FLEET UNDER ADMIRAL BREYA BLOWS UP ITS FIRST BUUTHANDI...

NOT PART OF THE CURRENT STORY, BUT DEFINITELY INTERESTING, YES?

Note: Regular readers no doubt know that "buuthandi" can be idiomatically tranlated to mean "Dyson sphere." Literally, it's the shortened form of the F'sherl-Ganni phrase "Buut go buut-buut nnaa-nnaa cho handi," or "this was expensive to build." (Transliterated, for the linguist: <Expensive and expensive-expensive [expletive] we built.>)

Regular readers may NOT know, however, that a buuthandi has more in common with a solar sail than with the conventional (and decidedly impractical) concept of a rigid Dyson sphere (Freeman Dyson's concept is not the conventionally impractical one, mind you. His idea will work). You see, the buuthandi does not support its own weight: it is essentially a balloon around a star, with power-collecting substations and giant habitats dangling from the inner surface. Control cables, millions of square kilometers of slack sail material, and some very clever engineering allow the 'balloon' to compensate for (and in some cases mitigate) the mood swings of the contained star.

This naturally begs the question: how do you blow one of these up? If it can stand up to a solar flare, it can certainly take a few planet-busting missiles.

There are a couple of ways to do this. The first involves convincing the contained star to go nova. The second involves using far, far more missiles than anyone thinks you can reasonably come up with. Either way, Admiral Breya has been busy.

QUEST FOR SECOND SIGHT PART III: THROUGH THE ROOF

THE TERAPORT WARS

53

Quest for Second Sight Part III: Through the Roof

Quest for Second Sight Part III: Through the Roof

CLOSE AIR SUPPORT

Feb 10, 2002

QUEST FOR SECOND SIGHT PART III: THROUGH THE ROOF

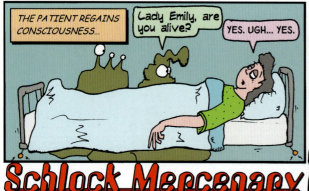

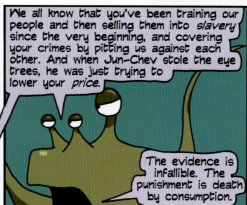

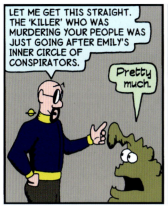

Quest for Second Sight Part III: Through the Roof

Note: Those concerned about test-firings of the orbital lance should keep a few things in mind. First, Sergeant Shodan's team is firing the weapon out of the plane of the Ghanj-Rho system, so it's not going to hit anything that anyone there cares about. Second, although the beam is gravitationally focused, and does perpetuate a braiding containment field as it progresses at just short of light-speed, it is not perfectly efficient, and it will eventually lose focus and become harmless. Oh, sure. It'll go a long, long way before dispersing, but the galaxy is made up of countless long, long ways, most of which are stacked end-to-end with very little actual matter thrown into the mix. Even then, the proportional amount of that matter that could be classified by entropy-resisting civilizations as 'point A,' or 'home,' or 'ground-zero' by virtue of something being there that matters to them is so close to zero that it makes next to no difference.

That said, two years after this test-firing, a 'dirty-snowball' cometary body (which had given rise to some slow-growing, anaerobic, single-celled organisms some kilo-millennia earlier) passed in front of the beam and was completely sterilized. Oh well. The comet was going to burn up in a star in another million years *anyway*, so it's not as if anything was actually lost. Think of it as a mercy-killing.

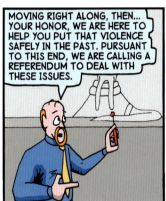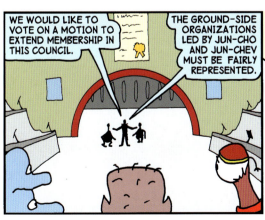

Quest for Second Sight Part III: Through the Roof

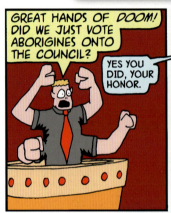

Quest for Second Sight Part III: Through the Roof

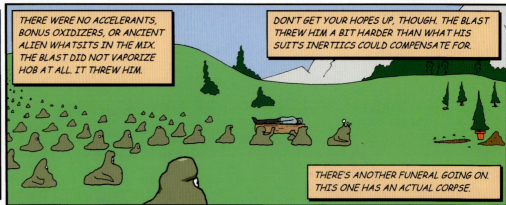

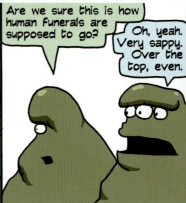
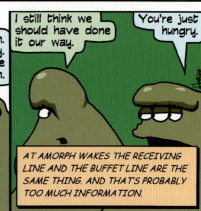

Epilogue: The blast that threw Corporal Hank "Hob" Obscromble through a wall and on a subsequent ballistic trajectory over three kilometers in length had one other effect. The hydraulic (for lack of a better term) shaft that channeled the blast was part of a pumping station (for lack of a better term) originally powered by microwaves beamed down from an enormous (that's actually a pretty good term) pre-annihilation-era powerplant on Ghanj-Rho's natural satellite.

The blast drove the machinery backwards for an instant, which had an understandably immeasurable effect on the tide-line of the artificial island it was built to keep afloat, since said island sank and was subsequently subducted with undersea crust movements some ten million (or so) years earlier. The thrust of the giant pistons did, however, send a tiny pulse of microwaves back to the well-preserved powerplant.

For a few minutes the lights inside burned brightly again, claiming for Hob what would have been third place for the "longest-ranged accidental death-lamp funeral service," had anyone from Frub-Xhin's Record-Setting Galactic Trivia actually been watching.

Quest for Second Sight Part III: Through the Roof

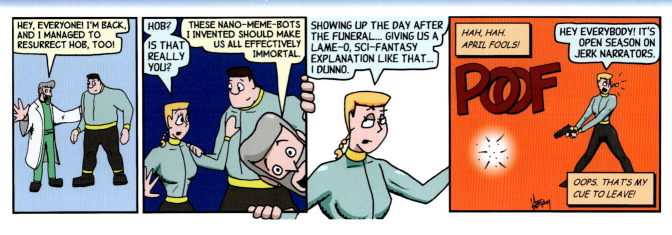

Artist commentary:

Designing Schlock was fairly easy. Designing a bunch of other amorphs to be visually distinguishable yet still obviously related was a bit of a challenge.

Okay, it really wasn't all that hard. I'm just trying to make it look like this is work.

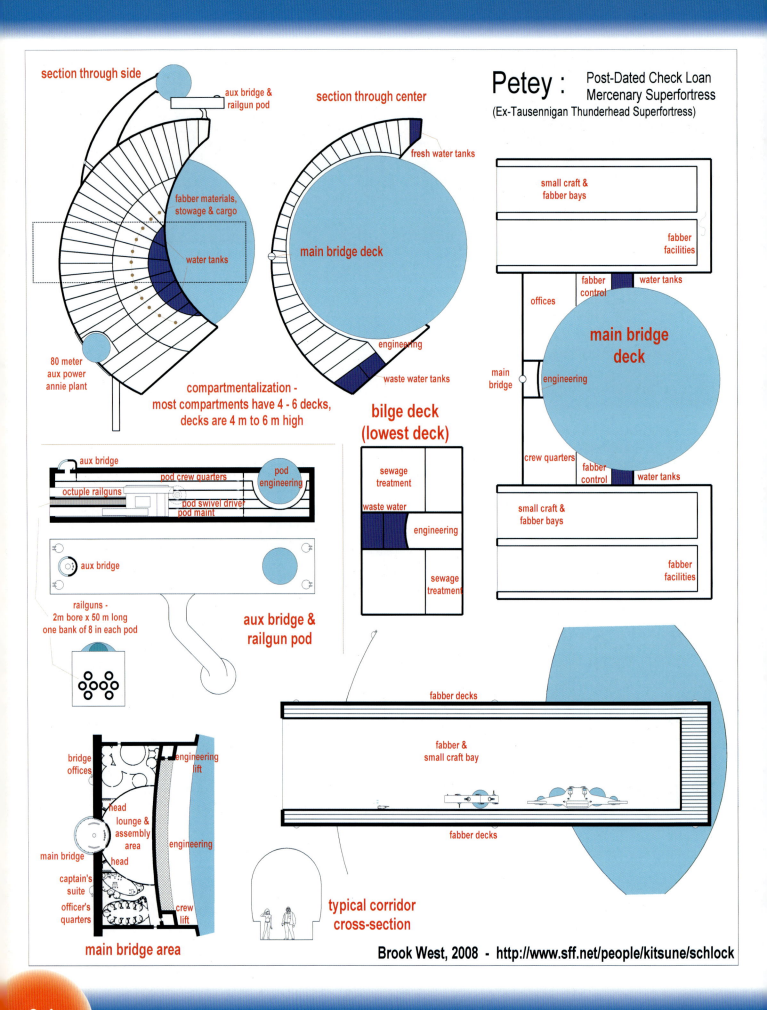

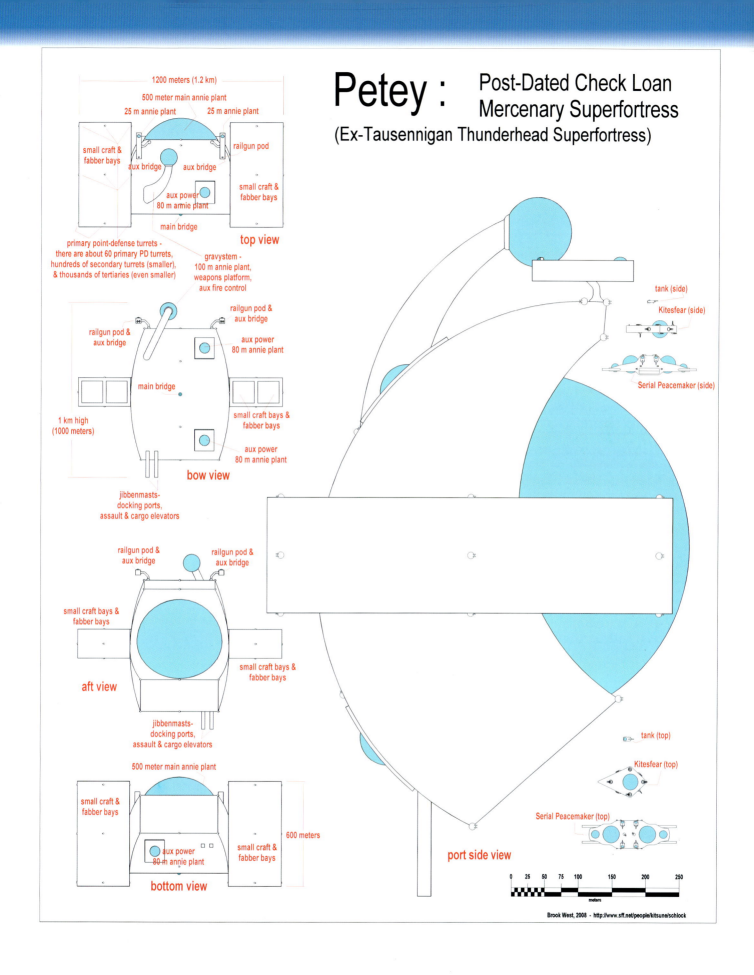

The Teraport Wars Part I: Kickin' Buuthandi and Takin' Names

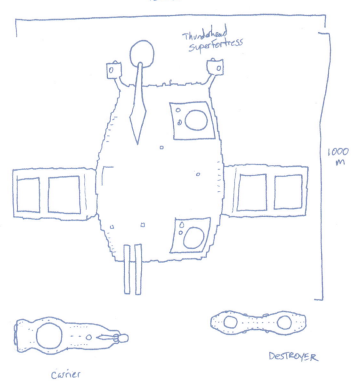

Prologue: Those reading *Schlock Mercenary* from the beginning might think they can just skip this bit, saying to themselves "oh, I know what already happened. I just want to see the picture. Why is this text here, anyway?" They'd be wrong. You see, although this prologue will make an obvious summary of previous events (the Toughs are in the Ghanj-Rho system, where they just finished finding new eyes for Sergeant Schlock, holding a funeral for Corporal Obscromble, and installing Rod the Bradicor into power, all in the space of about three weeks), it also provides some new information.

Not that any of it matters all that much. After all, most of you don't care that Rod has given a committee of five sophonts (a metisoid, a unioc, a big, pinkish bug-thing, and two amorphs) control of the Orbital Lance for continued defense of the station, as per the legislation that Lieutenant Massey Reynstein, J.D., drove through the council, nor are you concerned about the fact that the last of Lady Emily has been unceremoniously passed into the ecosystem outside of Tobir. You *might* be interested to know that very little time has passed since the funeral (hours, not days), but that kind of information may make it difficult for the small-minded to segment this new story from the old one.

Fortunately, readers of *Schlock Mercenary* are not small-minded. They're not entirely *normal*, but they're smart, smart people who are probably quite glad they read this entire prologue.

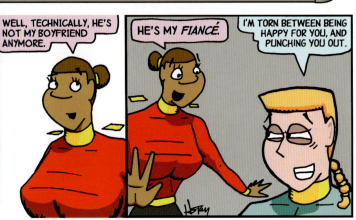

The Teraport Wars Part II: Kickin' Buuthandi and Takin' Names

The Teraport Wars

67

The Teraport Wars Part I: Kickin' Buuthandi and Takin' Names

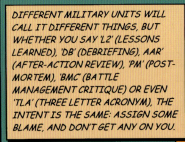

Schlock Mercenary

DIFFERENT MILITARY UNITS WILL CALL IT DIFFERENT THINGS, BUT WHETHER YOU SAY 'L2' (LESSONS LEARNED), 'DB' (DEBRIEFING), 'AAR' (AFTER-ACTION REVIEW), 'PM' (POST-MORTEM), 'BMC' (BATTLE MANAGEMENT CRITIQUE) OR EVEN 'TLA' (THREE LETTER ACRONYM), THE INTENT IS THE SAME: ASSIGN SOME BLAME, AND DON'T GET ANY ON YOU.

BEFORE WE BEGIN, KEVYN, I WANT TO MAKE SURE YOU KNOW THAT THE LOSSES WE HAD ON THIS OP WERE WELL WITHIN OPERATIONAL PARAMETERS.

THANK YOU, SIR.

ESPECIALLY CONSIDERING THAT THOSE PARAMETERS WERE DERIVED FROM 400 YEARS OF BELL-CURVE RESULTS FROM EVERY LOOSE-CANNONED NITWIT ON RECORD FOR COMMAND OF A SMALL FORCE IN HOSTILE TERRITORY. I THINK THAT YOU'D HAVE TO HAVE KILLED YOUR ENTIRE TEAM WITH YOUR BARE HANDS TO HAVE FALLEN OUTSIDE THEM.

OOOOH. THAT'S GONNA LEAVE A MARK.

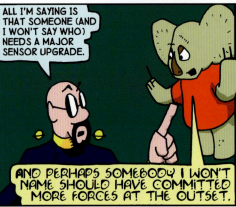

CAPTAIN, WE WOULD HAVE BEEN JUST FINE IF OUR BACKUP HAD BEEN TIMELIER.

HEY. YOU'RE GETTING READY TO BLAME ME FOR SOMETHING HERE.

ALL I'M SAYING IS THAT SOMEONE (AND I WON'T SAY WHO) NEEDS A MAJOR SENSOR UPGRADE.

AND PERHAPS SOMEBODY I WON'T NAME SHOULD HAVE COMMITTED MORE FORCES AT THE OUTSET.

YOU BOTH HAVE GOOD POINTS. THURL, LOOK INTO SENSOR UPGRADES FOR PETEY. KEVYN, YOU AND PETEY LOOK INTO FABBING SOME HEAVY ARMOR. START WITH, SAY, A FULL SQUADRON OF TANKS, AND THEN WORK YOUR WAY UP.

NEXT TIME WE GO INTO HARM'S WAY, I WANT MOST OF THE HARM TO BE WORKING FOR US.

SIR, I CAN ACQUIRE SENSOR PLANS ONLINE, AND I'M SURE WE CAN FEED THE FABBER AN ABANDONED BUILDING OR THREE, BUT WHAT ABOUT PERSONNEL?

WHAT DO YOU MEAN?

THE KIND OF FORCE YOU'RE TALKING ABOUT BEING ABLE TO DEPLOY IS AN ORDER OF MAGNITUDE LARGER THAN OUR ENTIRE COMPLEMENT OF GRUNTS AND SUPPORT STAFF.

WELL, MAYBE IT'S TIME TO START RECRUITING. WE HAVE AT LEAST ONE OPENING, AND I'M READY TO SEE SOME NEW FACES AROUND HERE.

YOU WANT ME TO KEEP TRACK OF THE ARTWORK ON *THREE HUNDRED* NEW FACES?

DO YOU HAVE *ANY IDEA* HOW DIFFICULT THAT IS?

I LET MYSELF IN. LISTEN, THAT LAST STORYLINE WAS PRETTY DRAINING, AND I WAS HOPING FOR A SPOT OF DOWN-TIME.

HEY, WHO LET YOU IN HERE?

EXCUSE US WHILE WE GET THE WHINEY AUTHOR OUT OF THE ROOM. PROPONENTS OF FOURTH WALL INTEGRITY WILL PLEASE JUST PRETEND THAT THESE LAST TWO PANELS NEVER HAPPENED.

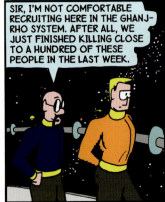

SIR, I'M NOT COMFORTABLE RECRUITING HERE IN THE GHANJ-RHO SYSTEM. AFTER ALL, WE JUST FINISHED KILLING CLOSE TO A HUNDRED OF THESE PEOPLE IN THE LAST WEEK.

THOSE WERE MOSTLY UNIOCS, RIGHT? STAY AWAY FROM UNIOCS, AND THEN RUN BACKGROUND CHECKS ON EVERYONE ELSE.

SIR, THE STATION HERE WAS FOUNDED AS A SAFE HAVEN FOR PRIVATEERS.

AND THAT MEANS THEY'RE OUR KIND OF PEOPLE, KEVYN.

THESE PEOPLE DON'T HAVE BACKGROUNDS. THEY HAVE CLEVERLY CONSISTENT ALIBIS.

THE TERAPORT WARS PART II: KICKIN' BUUTHANDI AND TAKIN' NAMES

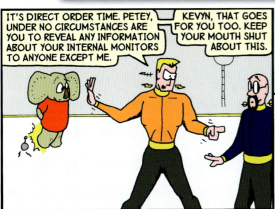

Note: There are several species of sophont here that we've not seen in *Schlock Mercenary* before, and a few that we have. From the head of the line to the back of the line, you're looking at a Unioc, a Fobottr, a Nejjat, a sub-bouncer-sized Vhorwed, Uklakk, a pink Wogni, another Unioc, an unimaginatively named Tetrisoid, and a Shla'al on his hover-stump. I'm not sure what the thing with the upside-down head is-- I suspect it's somebody's pet, but I could be wrong. Still, who is to say what's 'upside down' anyway? Depending on the length of its tongue, I expect it can lick its eyebrows in a way humans only fantasize about.

THE TERAPORT WARS

The Teraport Wars Part I: Kickin' Buuthandi and Takin' Names

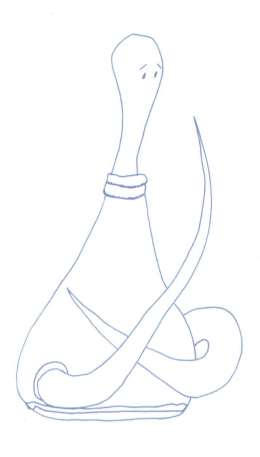
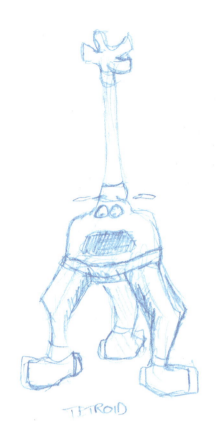

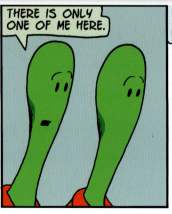

The Teraport Wars Part II: Kickin' Buuthandi and Takin' Names

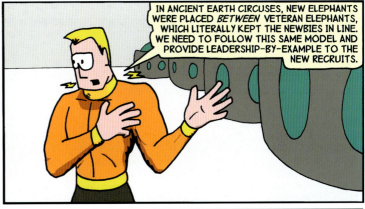

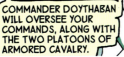

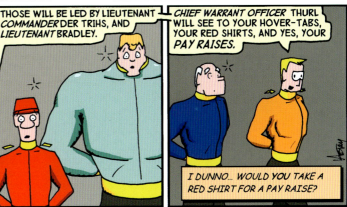

Note: For those of you confused by ranks in modern military organizations, it helps to know that they evolved out of pecking orders based primarily upon who was bigger than whom, and who could afford his own horse. With the parallel (but horribly out-of-sync) evolution of military technology and language, we find oxymorons like "general quarters" which is NOT where a general would be quartered, and "privates" who have so little personal privacy that their rank is an exercise in humorous irony. Fortunately, their pay is similarly humorous, so the joke works on multiple levels.

None of them currently own a horse. Slavery is illegal, after all.

The Teraport Wars Part I: Kickin' Buuthandi and Takin' Names

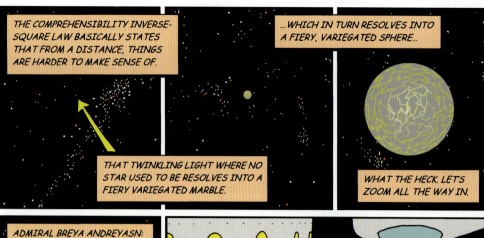

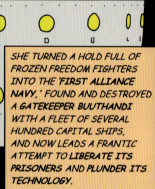
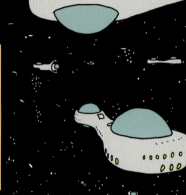
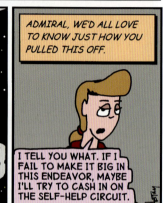

Note: While it is not, strictly speaking, necessary for the reader to page back to the beginning to understand what's going on, paging back to last year's Battle for the Wormgate story may provide some elucidating background information with a very healthy side-order of BLAM.

By way of summary, the 115,128 networked, civilized star systems of the 31st-century Milky-Way Galaxy (*population: 10,283 trillion and four. No... wait. Five. Err... three. Crap. Hold still.*) are connected by wormgates, which are run by the Gatekeeper Corporation. This corporation looks on the surface to be a friendly conglomerate of diverse races, but is actually managed by the F'Sherl-Ganni, a race of six-limbed, ten-handed goat-lizards that has been pulling strings for longer than humans have been walking upright.

Admiral Breya and her brother Kevyn inadvertently upset this age-old order of commerce by introducing a new hyperdrive that works independently of the wormgate network. One thing led to another (read that "people started killing people"), and now the Milky Way is in the throes of what 32nd-century historians and galacartographers will call "The Teraport Wars." (Interestingly, they'll look back on it as a colorful, yet statistically insignificant pimple on the face of history compared to the events that follow it, but let's not get ahead of ourselves.) In response to the chaos, and armed with insider knowledge about the F'Sherl-Ganni and the insidious side of their wormgates, Admiral Breya has undertaken a rather ambitious campaign to destroy their infrastructure and release their choke-hold on Galactic Society.

We'd mention here what the 32nd-century historians have to say about Breya's campaign, but it's much more interesting to live through history than to read about it (assuming, of course, that you actually live through it).

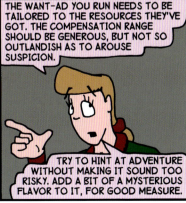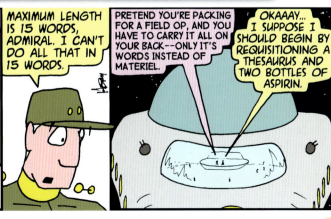

The Teraport Wars Part I: Kickin' Buuthandi and Takin' Names

THE TERAPORT WARS PART II: KICKIN' BUUTHANDI AND TAKIN' NAMES

Note: More than a few readers are still wondering why Breya has killed so many F'Sherl-Ganni by blowing up their buuthandi. The confusion arises from the popular (and rather absurd) image of a Dyson Sphere as something that provides lots of flat surface to live on. That's a silly image. Everything on the inside would fall into the central star, and everything on the outside would be cold and breathless, since there's too little solar gravity at that distance to hold down a proper atmosphere.

A buuthandi is like a balloon around a star, with space-stations dangling inward. In essence it's a solar sail in which the solar wind is precisely balanced with ballast. Breya's assault destroyed defensive facilities, and 'popped' the balloon, cutting it into segments. All of the habitat areas are intact, however, and only a very, very few F'Sherl-Ganni are dead (Vice-Lord Grak't'b'd'fwee having joined their fallen ranks recently). These habitats have dumped ballast and are sailing AWAY from the certain doom presented by falling into the central star, powered by giant sections of sail.

For an idea of the size of these sections of sail material, consider roadmaps. Start with one on which 1 centimeter equals 10 kilometers (a fairly common scale for useful maps). A map of your city and the surrounding countryside will fold up nicely in your hand. Now consider one where 10 kilometers equals 10 kilometers... to map your city on this, you'd need a piece of paper the size of your city.

Now consider one where, for some odd reason, you need even more detail. Like, you need 10,000 kilometers of map to represent a single kilometer of city streets. On this map you'll have mucking great avenues that represent cracks in the pavement. You could print a map like this for every city on Earth on a single, severed section of buuthandi sail material, and have room left over to gift-wrap Jupiter in enough layers that the recipient would have no idea what he was being given.

"Hmmm... it's really heavy. I give up, what did you get me?"

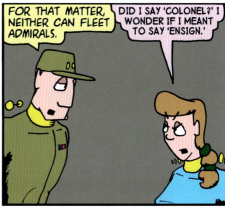

THE TERAPORT WARS

The Teraport Wars Part I: Kickin' Buuthandi and Takin' Names

THE TERAPORT WARS PART I: KICKIN' BUUTHANDI AND TAKIN' NAMES

Note: If you're wondering what exactly the math looks like, it's pretty complex. Basically, Newtonian formulae for acceleration due to gravity (plugging in the mass of the buuthandi's central star, and a distance of about 150,000,000 kilometers as a starting point for the prison modules) give us about 60 days before said modules burn up. Unfortunately, they were falling for just over a month before anyone noticed. A broken buuthandi is a big thing.

If we assume (horribly optimistically, but bear with me) that Petey can capture and offload one of these every 60 seconds, he will have saved some 40,000 of them before they start burning up. That leaves over four-point-nine-five MILLION of them plummeting into the furnace, and those are just in Petey's sector.

Even at less than a quarter full, these 950 million prison modules contain more than three times the population of early 21st-century Earth. To quote the thesaurus-impaired journalist, we have the makings of a "tragic tragedy of tragic proportions."

The Teraport Wars Part II: Kickin' Buuthandi and Takin' Names

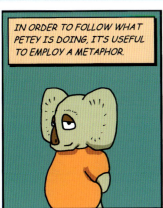

Note: Since I don't know what the smartest person you know actually looks like, I took some liberties in the strip above and drew myself. After all, with the glasses and the bald head and the beard, I look pretty smart. And hey, let's face it: today's strip is an excercise in imagination, *anyway*. You can *pretend* I'm the smartest person you know, can't you? Please? Just for today?

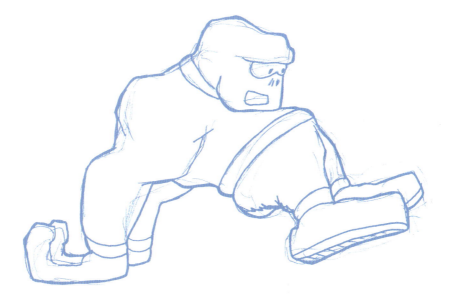

THE TERAPORT WARS

The Teraport Wars Part I: Kickin' Buuthandi and Takin' Names

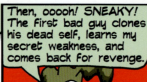

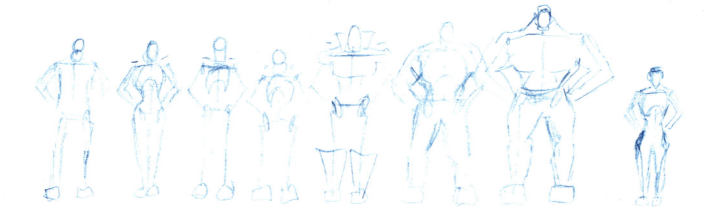

The Teraport Wars Part II: Kickin' Buuthandi and Takin' Names

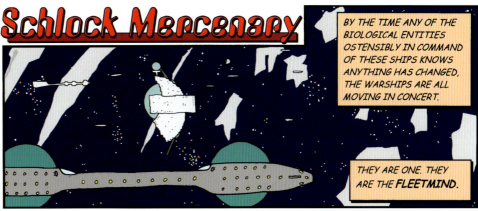

The Teraport Wars Part I: Kickin' Buuthandi and Takin' Names

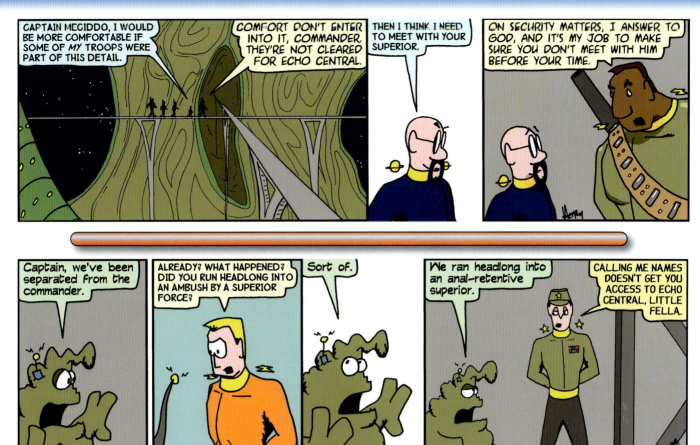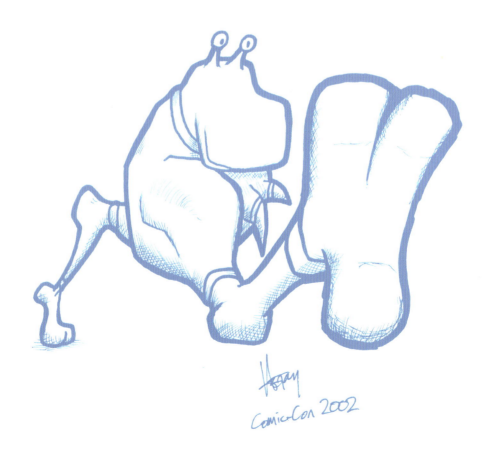

The Teraport Wars Part I: Kickin' Buuthandi and Takin' Names

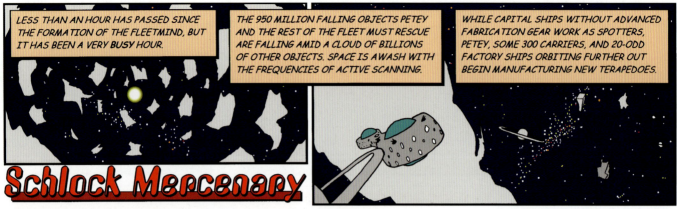

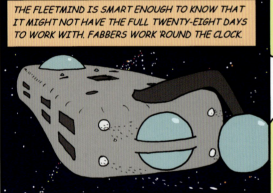

The Teraport Wars Part II: Kickin' Buuthandi and Takin' Names

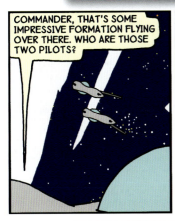

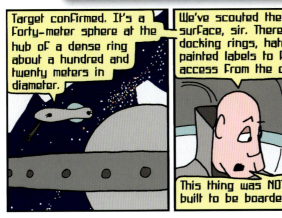

The Teraport Wars

85

The Teraport Wars Part I: Kickin' Buuthandi and Takin' Names

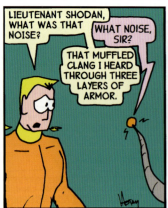

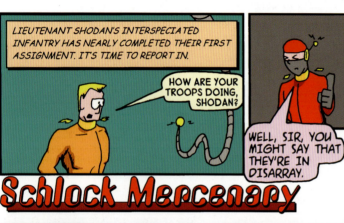

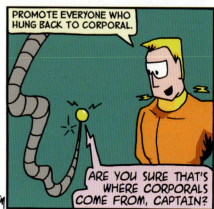

The Teraport Wars Part II: Kickin' Buuthandi and Takin' Names

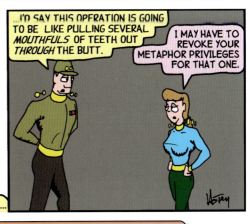

The Teraport Wars

The Teraport Wars Part I: Kickin' Buuthandi and Takin' Names

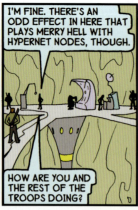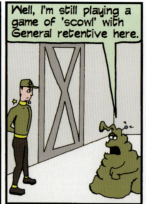
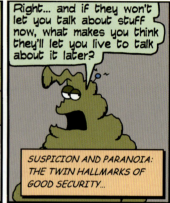

Artist commentary:

General Xinchub is seen here in an early, slimmer design, with epaulets I later discarded. Two-plus years after I drew this I shocked an audience at a convention in Austin Texas. They asked which character I most clearly identified with, and I told them it was Xinchub. Here was a guy who obviously wanted to do right by his constituents, and for whom the line between "good" and "evil" had become a broad, grey gradient. Me? I used to be in middle management at a large software company.

The Teraport Wars Part II: A Whole New Can O' Wormgates

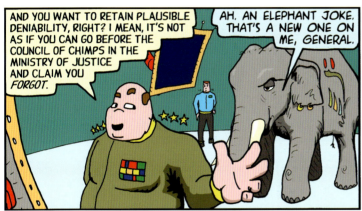

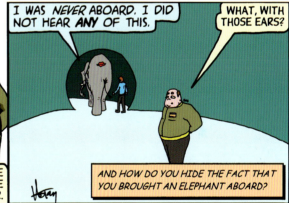

Note: Both Loxies (*Loxodontus Africanus Sapiens*) and Ellies (*Elephas Maximus Sapiens*, of which the Deputy Elephant is one) customarily adorn themselves with tatoos. Strictly speaking, they don't do it *themselves*, since the gene-twaddlers responsible for granting them sapience neglected to provide them with proper fingers, but who's keeping track? Regardless of which poorly-compensated body-artist is holding the needle, the practice is very widespread. Some say that sapient pachyderms adopted the custom as an alternative to wearing clothing, in order to better distinguish themselves from their dumb-as-stumps cousins. Others suggest that it's a concession to humans, most of whom can't tell the difference between a dog and four-point buck (as indicated by what gets shot at during the deer hunt), much less tell individual pachyderms apart.

It's hard to make it out, but the red smudge on the Deputy Elephant's ponderous behind is a stylized representation of a pair of lips. Pucker up, two-legs.

The Teraport Wars Part II: A Whole New Can O' Wormgates

Note: The handsome, blue-haired scientist is one of the oldest humans in the Galaxy, if you're counting from birthdates. Born in the late 20th century, "Gav" studied nuclear physics and worked for the government, but actually ended up making his fortune in the entertainment industry. In a quest to live to see the distant future, he had himself cryogenically frozen just prior to the Content Crash of the early 21st century. Thanks to the resultant depletion of his estate, he spent most of the next 1000-odd years being shuffled from one dusty, forgotten collegiate laboratory to another. He was thawed out by a teaching assistant in the late 31st century on the premise that "maybe this box labeled 'ancient biologicals' will have something nifty in it."

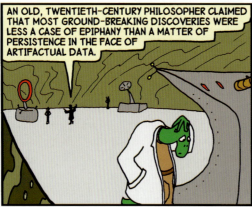

Note: The 'ancient philosopher' Gav is referring to is actually Isaac Asimov. Just so you know.

Nejjat Faces

The Teraport Wars Part II: A Whole New Can O' Wormgates

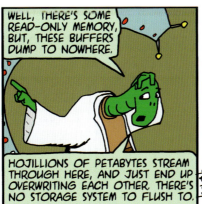

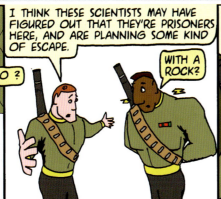

The Teraport Wars

The Teraport Wars Part II: A Whole New Can O' Wormgates

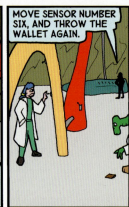

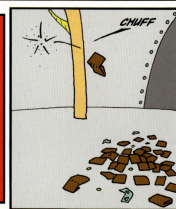

Note: Today's installment raises interesting questions about what this mini-gate is actually programmed to do. A wallet goes through intact, but an armored soldier with a multi-cannon strapped to his back is stripped naked? What's up with that?

First, it's helpful to note that this gate is not a travel-gate. It's more like an auxiliary input for the gate-copy system. Second, as you might imagine, some things are more dangerous than others. Guns and armor on a soldier are far more dangerous than a wallet (unless the wallet has large amounts of untraceable currency in it, and falls into the wrong [read that "my"] hands).

Third, the comedy inherent in a large, angry man being stripped naked over and over again, while being forced to watch the process and be embarrassed for himself in arithmetically increasing, serially experiential units of mortification is just too rich for words. Which, of course, is why we use *pictures* here at *Schlock Mercenary*.

The Teraport Wars Part II: A Whole New Can O' Wormgates

Note: Schlock's very first sewer adventure can be found in the Bonus Story at the end of this book, but we shan't spoil that for you... unless you want to turn straight to page 216.

The Teraport Wars Part II: A Whole New Can O' Wormgates

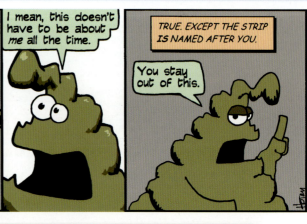

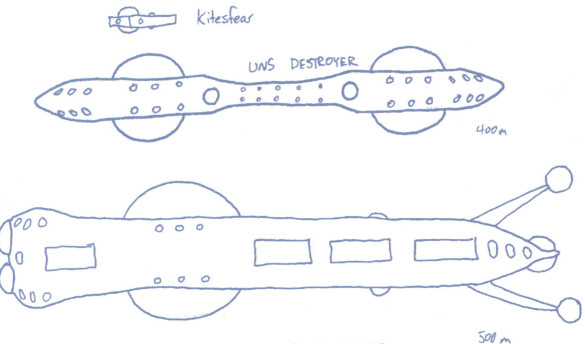

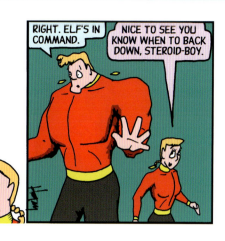

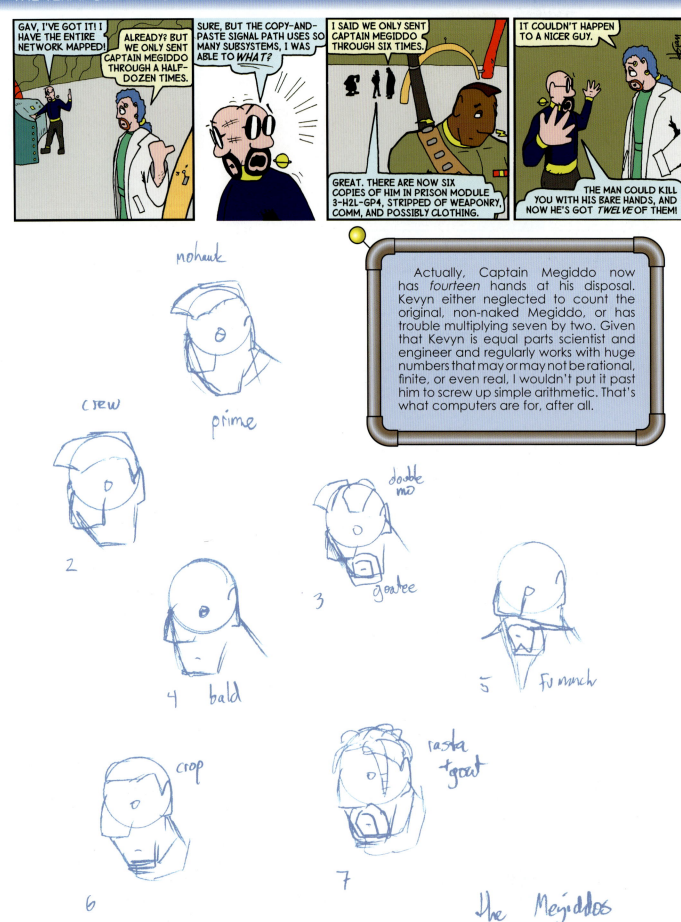

The Teraport Wars Part II: A Whole New Can O' Wormgates

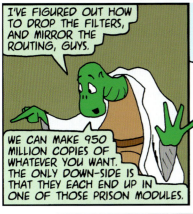

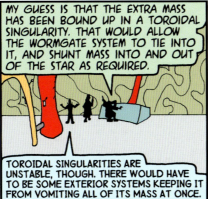
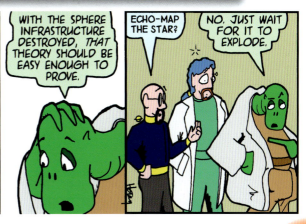

The Teraport Wars Part II: A Whole New Can O' Wormgates

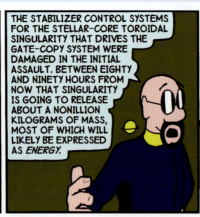

Note: In the strip above, Kevyn casually drops the number *a nonillion*, which to him means "a one followed by thirty zeroes." Many of you may not be aware, however, that a nice, specific number like that can actually have more than one meaning. The trouble stems from the fact that *a million* has six zeroes, and the original (and very sensible) meaning of *a billion* was "bi-million," which implies twice as many zeroes. Thus many Europeans hear Americans talking about "a billion-dollar aircraft," and wonder how the United States can afford to spend an entire GNP on something that flies quietly and drops bombs accurately, rather than only spending one or two milliard on it (yes, *a milliard* is a real number). Meanwhile, the scientific community has taken it upon themselves to adopt the American billion, which only has nine zeroes. Why did they adopt the American version, instead of the sensible version? Blame Hollywood. That's what I do, and it's no less useful than blaming someone with an actual conscience.

To add to the confusion, there are many even less specific "-illions" out there, like "*a bazillion*," which, I've been told, can be as high as 100,000,000 if you're counting jellybeans, and as low as 32 if you're counting, say, gunshot wounds.

The Teraport Wars Part II: A Whole New Can O' Wormgates

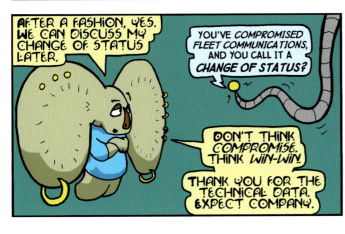

Note: Avid *Schlock Mercenary* archive-spelunkers may catch the fact that this is only the second strip in which Kevyn has shown us the face behind his glasses. They may also note that the last time we saw his eyes, they looked different. This is not a matter worthy of plot-oriented speculation. This is just a case of the "artist" opting to give Kevyn's eyes some whites, so that he can show more emotion, and so that the enemy will know when to open fire (in the unlikely event that Kevyn finds himself marching on an entrenched position without his glasses on).

Only those completely new to *Schlock Mercenary* will miss the change in Petey's ears. Unlike Kevyn's new eyeballs, this change is a matter worthy of plot-oriented speculation. Please do not email the author for hints, however. He is busily scripting opportunities for cast members to march on entrenched positions.

The Teraport Wars

The Teraport Wars Part II: A Whole New Can O' Wormgates

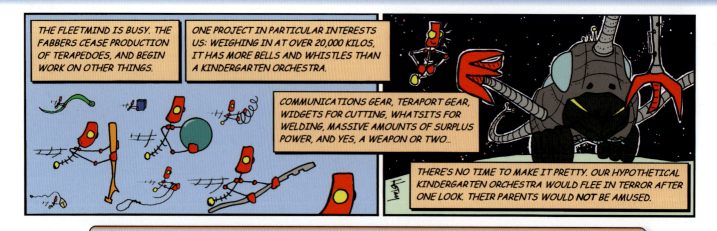

THE TERAPORT WARS PART III: F'SHERL-GANNI OR CUT BAIT

THE TERAPORT WARS

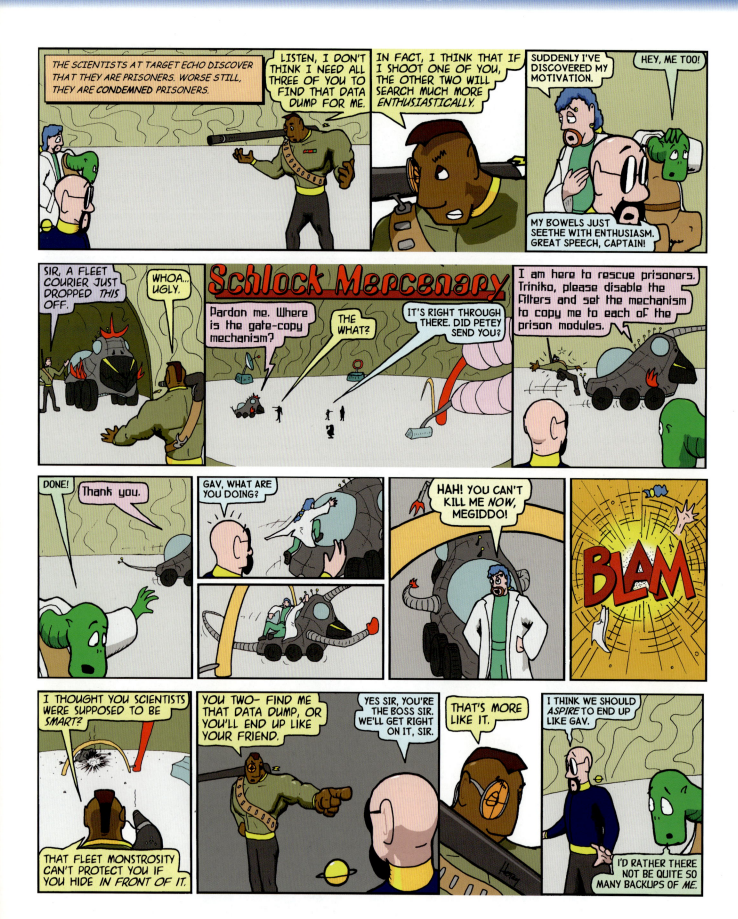

THE TERAPORT WARS PART III: F'SHERL-GANNI OR CUT BAIT

The astute reader may wonder whether or not the anti-tank breacher round Captain Megiddo turned loose at Gav was duplicated by the mini-gate. After all, we've established that Triniko, in order to allow the rescue-bot to be duplicated intact, has disabled whatever filtering mechanism prevents weapons, armor, and heat-resistant skivvies (such as those currently worn by one out of seven Megiddos) from being duplicated along with potential interrogatees. The consistency of the story hinges on little details like this, making such minutiae all that prevent *Schlock Mercenary* from being just a comic strip.

The challenge is that within the format of the comic strip, some story elements are necessarily omitted for clarity.

Missing from the opposite strip is a thirty-two-panel sequence featuring Triniko. Without going into too much detail, I'll say that it involves a flashback to her prior military experience in Nejjatese internecine border disputes. One occasion in particular haunts her -- she correctly judged the moment at which an enemy was going to open fire, but was frozen with fear and saw comrades perish as a result. While it may be difficult to imagine all this without actual pictures, per se, try to imagine how the panels build very climactically to the current moment when she realizes that Gav's plan to make himself safely redundant is doomed unless she can cut the filters back in line. The imagery as she throws the switch is powerfully symbolic (sadly, the feminists in the audience would likely offer a non-family-friendly interpretation of the symbolism implicit in a female grabbing an oblong, vertically-oriented switch in order to save the life of a male standing within an aperture from penetration by a missile fired from a rigid tube -- fortunately, there are no pictures, and said analysis will never get outside of these parentheses), and can even be said to be triumphant.

Since it would have been over twice as long as the panels currently in place, we've decided to give Triniko's flashback a wide miss, and just add this note. *Editor: cue the note now, please.*

Note: Megiddo's missile was not copied by the gate. We have Triniko's fast hands to thank for that.

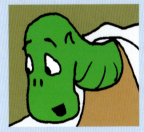

THE TERAPORT WARS

The Teraport Wars Part III: F'Sherl-Ganni or Cut Bait

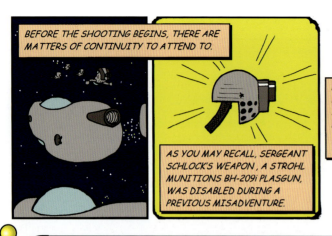

Note: With fabber technology available, it is not at all uncommon (and hardly surprising) for popular items like the trusty Strohl Munitions BH-series "Big Handguns" to be knocked off by scam artists trying to make a quick buck. It IS, however, uncommon for the knock-offs to be as good as the real thing. After all, in the galactic marketplace, anything worth making well is worth making LOTS of, so typically the brand-name manufacturers can make the genuine article for less than anyone else can.

Thus the importance of (and the legislation governing the use of) the logo. Sure, it's easy to manufacture a convincing logo right along with the rest of the item, but do you really want a weapons manufacturer upset at you for cutting in on their business? Some of their biggest customers may actually volunteer to help them track you down, lest your lower-quality gear fall into friendly hands and get someone hurt.

Naturally, none of this applies to Schlock's new weapon. Petey fabbed it for him, and 'cutting costs' was not on the agenda. Petey COULD have fabbed a logo to go right along with it, but he's a law-abiding warship (mostly), and figured Schlock would be just as happy without the logo as with the logo. If Schlock looks unhappy in the fourth panel, it's because he hasn't had a chance to FIRE the BH-250 yet. Once he's strapped it on and cut it loose he'll lose track of his 'logo-angst' in a euphoric orgy of plasmariffic destruction.

Addendum to note: The phrase "euphoric orgy of plasmariffic destruction" was plagiarized from the Strohl catalog, and appears on this site without permission. If they come looking for me, I was never here.

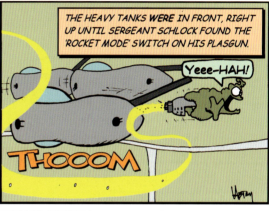

The Teraport Wars Part III: F'Sherl-Ganni or Cut Bait

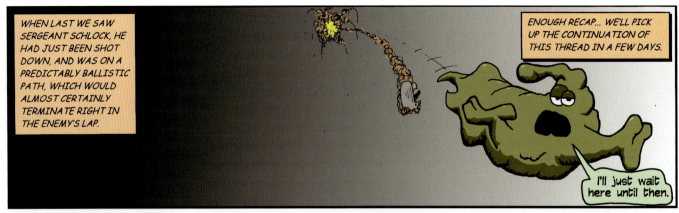

THE TERAPORT WARS PART III: F'SHERL-GANNI OR CUT BAIT

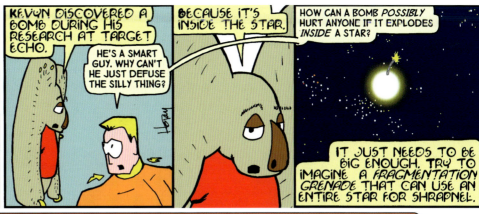

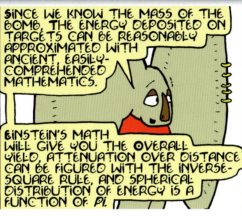

Note: It's fitting that we be treated to the description of a tremendous explosion on July 4th, when Americans everywhere are setting off explosions. It would have been even more fitting had the explosion actually been *featured* in today's strip, but we're not going to skip ahead in the storyline just to align the BLAM with a particular DATE.

(This raises an interesting question: what does the conversion of half a stellar mass sound like? After all, some sort of matter must be present for the wave-propagation effect that we think of as "sound" to occur. It's possible that the obliterated shell of stellar matter propelled outward by the blast would transmit kinetic energy in a way that could be percieved as noise, but after doing the math we suspect that it would hurt your ears. In fact, it would do so much damage to your hearing that we are inclined to misspell 'deafness' with the substitution of a second 'd' for that wholly unnecessary 'f.')

Hopefully this year's Independence Day celebrations will NOT feature even a SINGLE total-conversion bomb. Happy Birthday, America! Stand back when you light those fuses.

The Teraport Wars Part III: F'Sherl-Ganni or Cut Bait

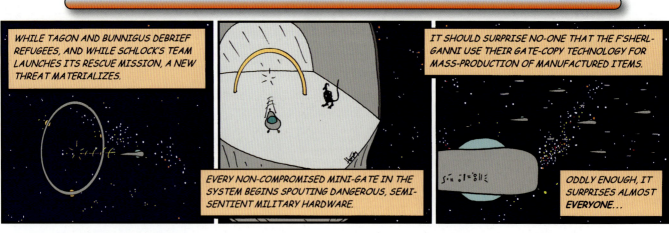

Aritst Commentary:

Newbie comic-book artists often fall into the trap of designing a monster or alien who is so cool, and so incredibly detailed that he's too time-consuming to draw regularly. For me, that was the F'Sherl-Ganni. I mean, come on! A guy who has a hard time drawing hands should not create an alien who has EIGHT OF THEM, and who can't gesture with just one at a time.

I think the discovery that they could "weave" their bifurcated forearms saved them from annihilation. It certainly meant I could put them in the strip more often. If you want to see what these critters should have looked like all the time, turn to p134.

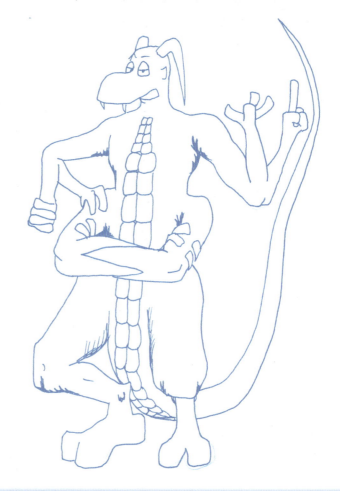

THE TERAPORT WARS PART III: F'SHERL-GANNI OR CUT BAIT

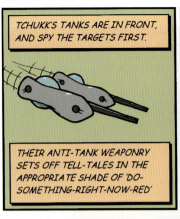

TCHUKK'S TANKS ARE IN FRONT, AND SPY THE TARGETS FIRST.

THEIR ANTI-TANK WEAPONRY SETS OFF TELL-TALES IN THE APPROPRIATE SHADE OF 'DO-SOMETHING-RIGHT-NOW-RED'.

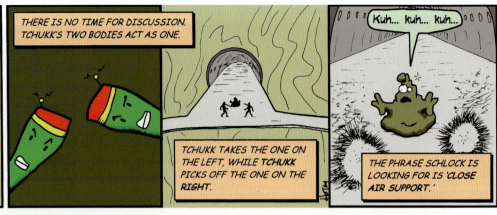

THERE IS NO TIME FOR DISCUSSION. TCHUKK'S TWO BODIES ACT AS ONE.

TCHUKK TAKES THE ONE ON THE LEFT, WHILE TCHUKK PICKS OFF THE ONE ON THE RIGHT.

Kuh... kuh... kuh...

THE PHRASE SCHLOCK IS LOOKING FOR IS 'CLOSE AIR SUPPORT.'

AS THE STRIKE TEAM REGROUPS BEFORE THEIR FINAL ASSAULT ON ECHO CENTRAL, THERE IS A BLAST, OF SORTS...

ANYONE WHO HAS SURVIVED A CLOSE ENGAGEMENT BETWEEN CAPITAL SHIPS KNOWS THE SENSATION — GRAVY GUNS ARE BEING FIRED NEARBY.

THE REFERENTIAL SHEAR IMPLICIT IN CONFLICTING GRAVITY GRADIENTS IS QUITE UNMISTAKABLE. IF YOU'VE LIVED THROUGH IT, IT MEANS THE ENEMY MISSED, OR THE DAMPERS ON YOUR OWN GRAVY GUNS HAVE JUST PASSED THEIR 'SELL-BY' DATE. CONFLICTING FORCES THREATEN TO TEAR YOU ASUNDER, WHILE TELLING YOUR INNER EAR THAT NOW WOULD BE A GOOD TIME TO HAVE A SIT-DOWN. THE SENSATION IS A LITTLE LIKE FALLING BETWEEN A DANCING PAIR OF F3 TORNADOES, ONLY WITHOUT QUITE SO MANY COWS...

BHYUUICK

IF YOUR LAST MEAL WAS STANDARD SHIPBOARD PAP, YOU'LL SOON SEE EXACTLY WHY THEY CALL THESE 'GRAVY GUNS.'

Did you feel that!?! They've got gravy guns!

BIG ONES, TOO. THESE TANKS ARE NO PROTECTION AGAINST A POWER SOURCE THAT SIZE.

Then let's get moving! Kevyn doesn't have protection from a gun that big, either.

HEH. WHADDAYA WANNA BET HE BUILT IT? OUT OF SPARE PARTS, NO LESS.

Well, if he's firing it indoors, he needs help. In more ways than one.

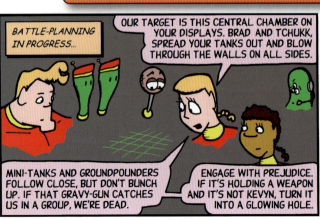

BATTLE-PLANNING IN PROGRESS...

OUR TARGET IS THIS CENTRAL CHAMBER ON YOUR DISPLAYS. BRAD AND TCHUKK, SPREAD YOUR TANKS OUT AND BLOW THROUGH THE WALLS ON ALL SIDES.

MINI-TANKS AND GROUNDPOUNDERS FOLLOW CLOSE, BUT DON'T BUNCH UP. IF THAT GRAVY-GUN CATCHES US IN A GROUP, WE'RE DEAD.

ENGAGE WITH PREJUDICE. IF IT'S HOLDING A WEAPON AND IT'S NOT KEVYN, TURN IT INTO A GLOWING HOLE.

My glowing-hole-maker got blown up. What am I supposed to turn targets into?

LUNCH, PERHAPS? I'VE SEEN YOU EAT.

Aww, you're just sweet on me, Elf.

The Teraport Wars Part III: F'Sherl-Ganni or Cut Bait

QUESTION: HOW DO YOU KEEP AN AMORPH ENTERTAINED WHEN THE ONLY HEAVY WEAPONS ON HAND ARE ATTACHED TO YOUR TANK?

ANSWER: LET HIM RIDE ON TOP.

"Hey Ennesby, this barrel is getting awfully warm."

"That's because I didn't think you'd appreciate me firing up the heat-sink laser while you're sitting on it."

Artist commentary:
Remember what I said about colored pencils back on page nine? I rest my case. But if you flip back to page nine you'll see that I'd become a better artist by p111 here. You can tell because I positioned Tagon so that you can actually see his hands.

The Teraport Wars

111

The Teraport Wars Part III: F'Sherl-Ganni or Cut Bait

Note: The most accurate galactic census data is compiled by HeadCount Incorporated, which is a wholly-owned subsidiary of The Wormgate Corporation. HeadCount Incorporated performs censuses on the 115,128 star systems officially connected to Wormgates, and at last count showed just over 10,200 trillion sophonts from 203,175 different sapient species. Humans, prolific procreators by almost anyone's standards, account for around one person in 10,000.

HeadCount Incorporated does not, however, perform censuses on the gatekeepers themselves. The F'Sherl-Ganni, were they to allow census-takers into all of their buuthandi, would rocket past Humanity and three other species to claim the #1 spot with 54 trillion sophonts.

Those readers curious for more detailed information (like the list of the top five most populous species in the Galaxy, or the number of actual 31st-century people who still read webcomics) are encouraged to subscribe to HeadCount Incorporated's *Galactic Demographics Weekly**.

*Hypernet service required. For more information, contact a hypernet service provider near you.

The Teraport Wars Part III: F'Sherl-Ganni or Cut Bait

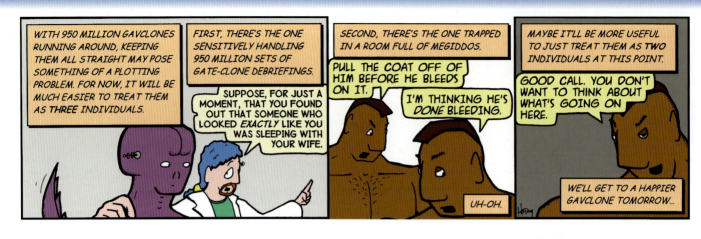

Anatomy

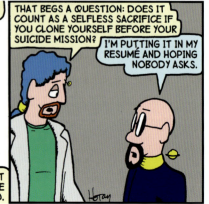

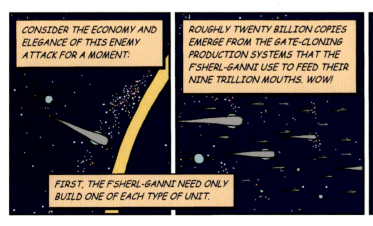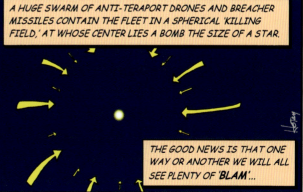

The Teraport Wars Part IV: Any Teraport in a Storm

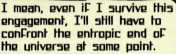

The Teraport Wars Part IV: Any Teraport in a Storm

Schlock Mercenary

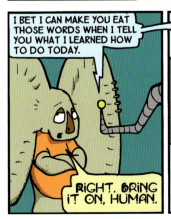
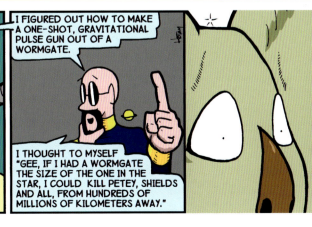

The Teraport Wars Part IV: Any Teraport in a Storm

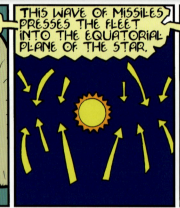

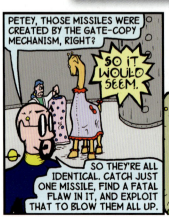

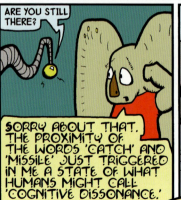

The Teraport Wars Part IV: Any Teraport in a Storm

The Teraport Wars Part IV: Any Teraport in a Storm

Schlock Mercenary

The Teraport Wars Part IV: Any Teraport in a Storm

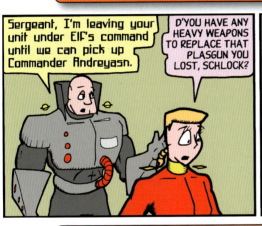

The Teraport Wars

The Teraport Wars Part IV: Any Teraport in a Storm

Kevyn! It's good to see you in one piece.
HALFWAY DOWN THE WESTERN SPIRAL ARM, THERE IS A REUNION IN PROGRESS.

SO YOU SAW WHAT HAPPENED AFTER I COPIED MYSELF?
Just the results. Very messy.
BUT IT WORKED, RIGHT?

There was an unholy gouge running the length of the room, and all the bad guys were, well, sort of splattered.
HAH! I'M A GENIUS!

You were pretty dead, too, you know.
MY NEW FIRST RULE OF ADVANCED WEAPON TESTING: MAKE A BACKUP OF YOURSELF BEFORE OPENING FIRE.

ABOARD THE MERCENARY SUPERFORTRESS 'POST-DATED CHECK LOAN' PLANS ARE PUT INTO MOTION. DANGEROUS PLANS...
MOVE, PEOPLE! THIRTY SECONDS!

Schlock Mercenary

SCANS SHOW WE'RE CLEAR, CAPTAIN. SEAL UP, AND SIT TIGHT.
ROGER THAT, PETEY. EVERYONE IS ACCOUNTED FOR.

HOW LONG IS THIS MISSILE DRILL GOING TO TAKE, CAPTAIN? I'VE GOT A CAKE GOING THAT NEEDS ATTENTION.
THAT DEPENDS ON HOW THE DRILL GOES, SERGEANT.

IF WE BOTCH THE MISSILE DRILL, WE'LL BE TRYING OUT THE 'DAMAGE CONTROL' DRILL, AND I'M WILLING TO BET YOU'LL HAVE TO JUST WRITE OFF THAT CAKE ALTOGETHER.

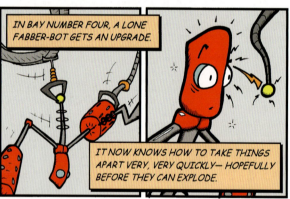
IN BAY NUMBER FOUR, A LONE FABBER-BOT GETS AN UPGRADE.
IT NOW KNOWS HOW TO TAKE THINGS APART VERY, VERY QUICKLY— HOPEFULLY BEFORE THEY CAN EXPLODE.

CAPTAIN, THE DRONES HAVE ISOLATED A MISSILE. I'M BRINGING IT IN NOW.
CAPTAIN, ABOUT THIS DRILL... SHOULD I BE PRAYING FOR... UM... SUCCESSFUL DRILLING?
THAT SOUNDS LIKE AN EXCELLENT IDEA. JUST MAKE THEM FAST PRAYERS.

THE BREACHER MISSILE IS MADE TO THINK IT'S NOT THROUGH THE SHIELDS YET. THE COMPLEX GRAVITICS IN BAY FOUR FOOL IT LONG ENOUGH FOR FABBY TO GET IN CLOSE WITH HIS NIFTY NEW SET OF TOOLS...

KA-BOOM
ALAS, POOR FABBY. WE HARDLY KNEW THEE.
SORRY, CH'VORTHQ. SOUNDS LIKE WE'LL BE BUSY FOR A WHILE YET.
OH IT'S NO TROUBLE. I BET MY CAKE FELL, ANYWAY.

The Teraport Wars Part IV: Any Teraport in a Storm

Hotay
July 8th, 2002

The Teraport Wars Part IV: Any Teraport in a Storm

The Teraport Wars

The Teraport Wars Part IV: Any Teraport in a Storm

Note: *T'okjith* is yet another F'Sherl-Ganni contraction that carries far more meaning than any pair of syllables should. Contextually, it means "dangerous, barely-controlled singularity," and is used to refer to the toroidal singularity at the heart of a *buuthandi*'s central star. The complete phrase from which the contraction was derived, "*Taana ok, en cho jith dan breeka cho braa'ka cho Ganni ti ips'aa ta baala dinka-cho fatu jith,*" can be idiomatically translated as "The design is clever, but this <expletive> thing could sterilize a sizeable <expletive> chunk of the <expletive> galaxy if you're not <expletive> careful with it."

This particular phrase would not have been memorable (and certainly would not have been condensed and conjuncted and turned into a single word) had the speaker and 99% of his audience not been vaporized by a *T'okjith* that someone was not *dinka-cho* careful with.

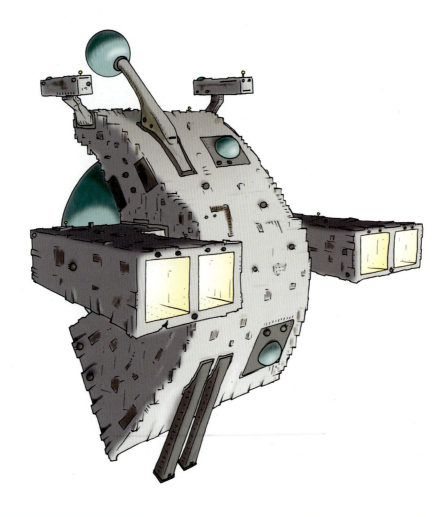

THE TERAPORT WARS PART IV: ANY TERAPORT IN A STORM

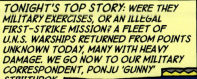
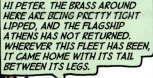

THE TERAPORT WARS

The Teraport Wars Part IV: Any Teraport in a Storm

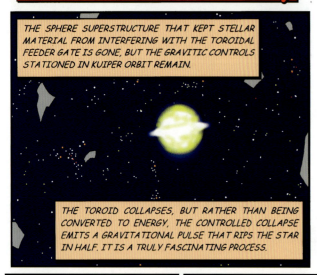

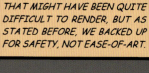

Epilogue: Send in the Clones

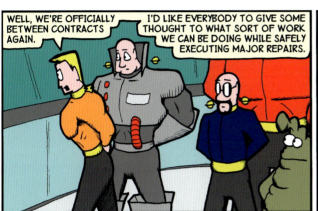

Epilogue: Send in the Clones

Note: While it may seem harsh that the 31st-century equivalent of "Driving Under the Influence" carries with it the death penalty, this is due to an inherent *in*equivalency between MOUI and DUI.

With DUI, you need only climb into your vehicle while under the influence of alchohol or drugs and attempt to drive it home.

With MOUI you must disable a number of safety systems designed to prevent idiots like you from manually operating their vehicles while inebriated, overtired, wasted, decaffeinated, angry, emotionally distraught, or suffering from hormonal disorders like PMS or testosterone poisoning (the latter having been positively identified as a leading cause of stupidity among males between the ages of puberty and death). After disabling the safety systems (which task almost certainly requires ice-cold sobriety), you must decide to switch the vehicle to a manual mode of operation. In some cases, this requires *installing* a manual mode of operation.

After this demonstration of superior technical skills and poor judgement, you must then deliberately impair your defective judgement further by quaffing, inhaling, injecting, or otherwise consuming something mildly toxic (or, in some precedent-setting cases, breaking up with your girlfriend.)

At this point you might argue that you are no longer responsible for your actions, which actions include climbing into your vehicle and attempting to pilot it home. Technically, this is true. The prosecution will counter by arguing that it isn't Manual Operation Under the Influence that you are going to be humanely (if rather publicly) executed for. It's the fact that you deliberately made such an irresponsible act POSSIBLE by putzing around with your ride. You know those signs that say "don't putz around with this system -- serious injury or death could result?" Well, they were talking about YOUR death, and it is now resulting.

Epilogue: Send in the Clones

April 15, 2008

Epilogue: Send in the Clones

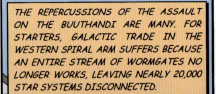

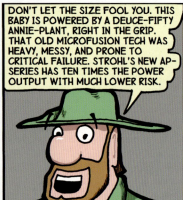

Epilogue: Send in the Clones

Note: One of the most respected works regarding the F'Sherl-Ganni, the Wormgate Network, and the Teraport Wars, is also the most mysterious. *The Tinth-Philkra Dialogues* was published anonymously and is a collection of supposedly factual conversations. Historians fall into one of two camps regarding the *Dialogues*: either they consider 90% of the material little more than well-thought-out historical fiction, or they see it as a collection compiled by a shadowy conspiracy of key players.

The Tinth-Philkra Dialogues hit the hypernet from the Tinth III node in the Philkra system (hence the name) shortly after the flagship *Athens*, the frigate *Sarasota*, and two Nejjat shuttles disappeared, but they contain dialogues that would have been unknown to Admiral Breya, Commodore Haban II, or any of their staff. Conversations between Generals Xinchub and Aanders, Admiral Breya and Captain Tagon, Sixth-Lord p'd'k'Tag and Master g'd'p'Tawn, Gav2906351 and Triniko, and Hizzoner the Right Reverend Choka Mbutu and the First Assistant to the Deputy Elephant of the United Nations are all featured, and no common link among these individuals has ever been identified.

One utterly discredited theory suggests that the Fleetmind recorded each of the dialogs somehow, and dumped them into a repository prior to disbanding. The fact that this discreditation was executed with the help of ex-Fleetmind units has unfortunately not been the subject of sufficiently rigorous study.

THE TERAPORT WARS

Laura Hoerster
http://laurasketches.blogspot.com/

PETEY PROMOTED: SAWED OFF SCHLOCK GUN

Prologue: For those in need of a quick recap before beginning this next chapter in the ongoing *Schlock Mercenary* comic opera, here goes -- Our heroes (a band of mostly scrupulous mercenaries aboard an oversized sentient starship) have just completed a stint with an ad-hoc fleet bent on waging war with the most powerful economic force in the Galaxy, the F'Sherl-Ganni, who control the network of wormgates that used to be the only way to get around.

One result of that tour of duty was severe damage to the port bays of the mercenary superfortress *Post-Dated Check Loan*. Another result was the destruction of Sergeant Schlock's *third* BH-series plasgun, whose delightfully deterrent *ommminous hummm* is still being missed.

For those not in need of a quick recap, and who expect these purely textual additions to Schlock Mercenary to have a punchline of sorts, you're out of luck. The only punchline available is in the strip below.

THE TERAPORT WARS

Petey Promoted: Sawed off Schlock Gun

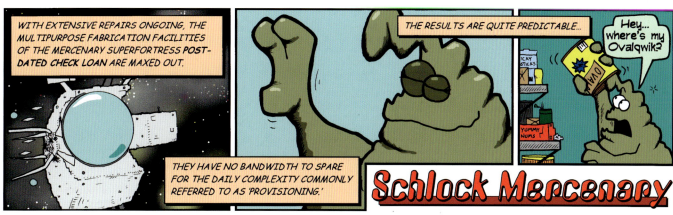

Petey Promoted: Filling the Tub of Happiness

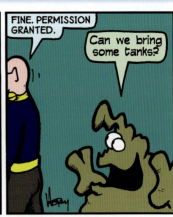

PETEY PROMOTED: FILLING THE TUB OF HAPPINESS

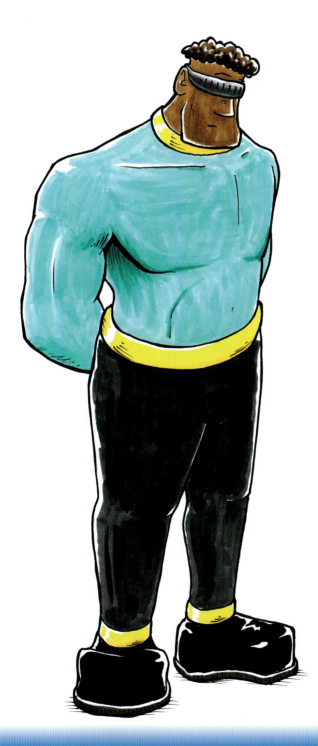

Artist commentary:

I suppose it was racially insensitive of me to design my very first dark-skinned character wearing goggles like those worn in *Star Trek: The Next Generation* by LeVar Burton... who is also the guy who played Kunta Kinte in *Roots*. If I owe an apology to anyone, however, it's Shep here. He really deserves his own story, and he's not getting it in this book.

THE TERAPORT WARS

PETEY PROMOTED: FILLING THE TUB OF HAPPINESS

Note: Before the detail-oriented *Schlock Mercenary* readership jumps all over the author about mis-stating Lieutenant *Commander* Der Trihs' rank, it should be known that Der Trihs still gets little respect from the crew, even after his promotion following his utter non-participation in the events in *Ghanj-Rho*. You can hardly expect the enlisted men errr... things to use his full title when dissing him behind his back.

We should also note that the *Post-Dated Check Loan* is not listing to starboard because that side is 'heavier.' The visual imbalance implicit in the missing port-side bays has nothing to do with the angle of display in the first panel. I mean, it might LOOK like the *P.D.C.L.* is heavier on one side, and that might SEEM like it would make it tip a bit, but if I have to explain to you why that's not really the case, we'll be here all day.

PETEY PROMOTED: FILLING THE TUB OF HAPPINESS

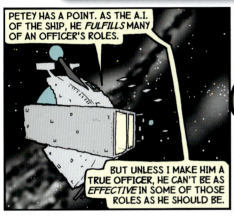

THE TERAPORT WARS

Petey Promoted: Filling the Tub of Happiness

Petey Promoted: Filling the Tub of Happiness

Petey Promoted: Filling the Tub of Happiness

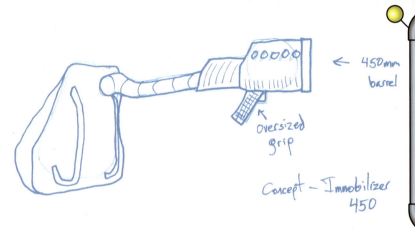

Note: The Immobilizer 450 obtained its numerical designation from the same place it obtained its appeal -- the muzzle diameter. At nearly half a meter around, it looks more like a place to hide than something you'd get shot with. (Important safety tip: never ever hide in the barrel of an Immobilizer 450).

Schlock Mercenary

Petey Promoted: Filling the Tub of Happiness

Note: Those of you wondering where Chuk's goggles went, or worrying about the possibility of asphyxiation of a target struck by immobilizer fire, will be pleased to learn that the answers are related. The green-mod goober rounds in use by Schlock's team are mildly nanomotile in nature, and can detect buildups of gases related to the most common types of respiration. Shots covering a respiratory opening will migrate away, allowing the target to breathe and, in some cases, see (there are sapient species with eyes in their 'mouths' or 'nostrils,' although it's equally accurate to say that they eat and/or breathe with their eye-sockets). Thus, Chuk got shot in the face, and the goober-goo migrated off of his face, and took his goggles with it.

The nanomotile nature of goober-goo also helps ensure target immobility and maximum discomfort. Green-mod 30 will actually give wedgies, and it's impolite to talk about what green-mod 19 will do.

The Teraport Wars

PETEY PROMOTED: FILLING THE TUB OF HAPPINESS

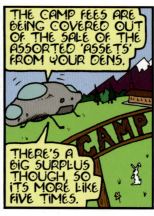

PETEY PROMOTED: SCHLOCKTOBERFEST 2002

Prologue: Today's strip begins a new tradition -- *Schlocktoberfest,* in which Schlock Mercenary takes a turn for the dark side for 31 days or so. Oh, you might think that LAST October was when the tradition began, but as everyone knows, it's not a tradition until you do it the second time.

By way of recapitulation, the A.I. of the mercenary superfortress *Post Dated Check Loan* has recently been granted officer status (Probationary Special Lieutenant), and in that capacity managed to plan one of the most successful missions the Toughs have ever carried off. The fact that this calls into question the relative capabilities of every other officer ever to plan a mission for the company has yet to draw any attention, which itself calls into question the relative capabilities of every other officer ever to plan a mission for the company.

The fact that we escaped that last paragraph without recursion is further evidence that the word 'genius' may not be too strong a word to describe the author. Since 'cocky' and 'schmuck' are also in this category, we'll not pursue this line of reasoning further...

THE TERAPORT WARS

Petey Promoted: Schlocktoberfest 2002

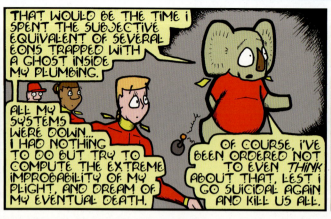

Petey Promoted: Schlocktoberfest 2002

Schlock Mercenary

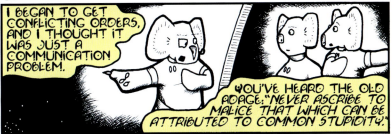

The Teraport Wars

Petey Promoted: Schlocktoberfest 2002

Note: Kssthrata 'troops' are often referred to as 'teeth'-- it's a cultural thing. This is reflected in their ranks, as well: 'Foretooth' is the equivalent of 'column leader,' which term evolved into 'colonel' on ancient Earth.

One might wonder at the rank of 'sergeant' which in English (and hence the corrupted Galstandard West) originated from the latin word for 'servant' and through the passage of centuries went from meaning 'soldier-servant of a knight' to meaning 'I am your momma, your poppa, and your shoulder to die on.'

In the Kssthrata tongue the word has a different (albeit rather parallel) history, and stems from the tooth-related word "serrator" and the word "gentle(man)." Literally, the rank of sergeant among the Kssthrata is the leader of the 'serrator' troops, or 'gent responsible for serrating our enemies.'

A kindly gent indeed.

Petey Promoted: Schlocktoberfest 2002

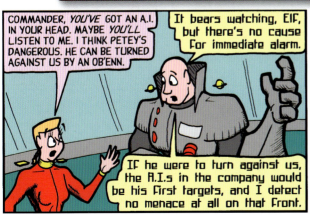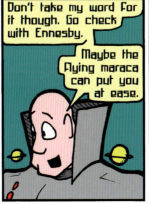

Petey Promoted: Schlocktoberfest 2002

Petey Promoted: Schlocktoberfest 2002

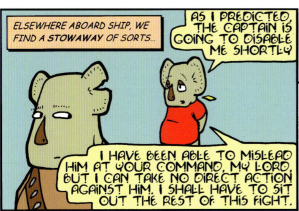

Note: Petey's mass, according to Captain Tagon, is "a few million tons." It would be more accurate to say "a few *hundred* million metric tons." It's difficult to be more precise without enumerating starting conditions -- how much neutronium is in each of the Annie-Plants, how far along is the reconstruction of bays three and four, and so forth.

In the spirit of challenging the reader, here's an easy one: If Petey displaces as much water as a heavier-than-water sphere of 1000 meters diameter, what's the LEAST he can weigh? (And don't give me any excuses along the lines of "things in space don't weigh anything." If he's displacing water, we can safely assume he's not in space. Think Earth-normal gravity, you bozos.)

If that problem's not difficult enough for you, here's a hard one: extrapolate Petey's blueprints and superstructure from the drawings in the comic, estimate the mass of the hypertensile materials with which he's constructed, average out the mass of his fittings and crew, and tell us all how much of the rest of his mass is neutronium.

Show your work.

Petey Promoted: Schlocktoberfest 2002

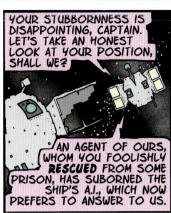

Note: If you're wondering what the Admiral is referring to when he says that Tagon rescued an Ob'enn agent from prison, he's obviously talking about the fact that Tagon took a number of gate-cloned prison refugees aboard. See if you can find the Ob'enn in the first strip on page 108. It's easier than "Where's Waldo," and there are fewer of those annoying stripes.

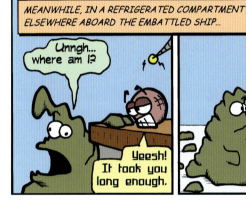

Artist commentary:

By the time I got to the final outline of this story the scene depicted to the right had been cut. I liked it so much, though, that I used this idea in the third panel on p.149.

The Teraport Wars

Petey Promoted: Schlocktoberfest 2002

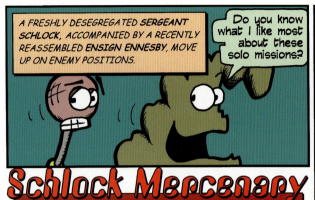

Artist Commentary:
I love fabbies. We'll see more of them.

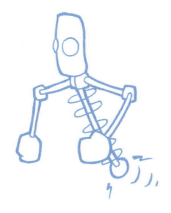

Petey Promoted: Schlocktoberfest 2002

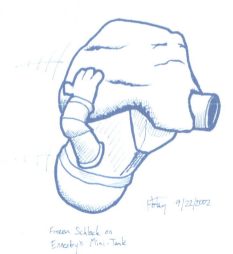

Frozen Schlock on Ennesby's Mini-Tank

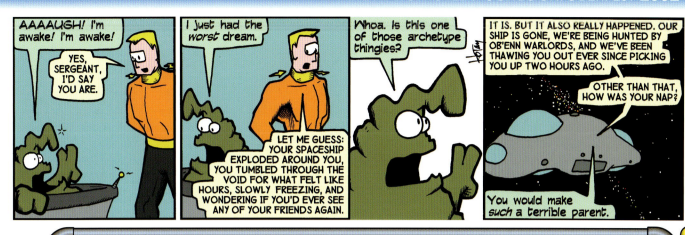

Note: Sure, sure... we *could* have done a week's worth of strips detailing the frantic game of hide-and-go-teraport around Planet Chuba, as Tagon and company sought not only to elude the angry Ob'enn light craft, but also to locate their tumbling, freezing comrade. It was a race against time, for had the sergeant tumbled out of the shadow of Chuba into the raw, harsh starlight of space, he would have been cooked.

Why did we decide not to build comics around this story? Well, it's not October anymore. *Schlocktoberfest* is therefore over, and the proposed story title "The Search for Schlock" had too creepy a ring to it.

Kevin Wasden
www.splintered-mind.com

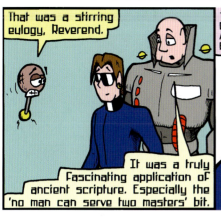

Post Post-Dated Check Loan Part I: Raising Capital Offensive

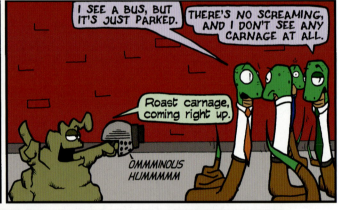

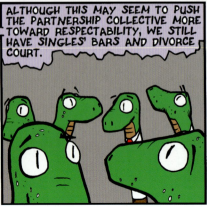

POST POST-DATED-CHECK-LOAN PART I: RAISING CAPITAL OFFENSIVE

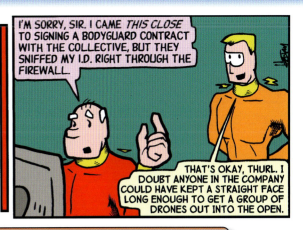

THE TERAPORT WARS

POST POST-DATED CHECK LOAN PART I: RAISING CAPITAL OFFENSIVE

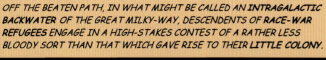

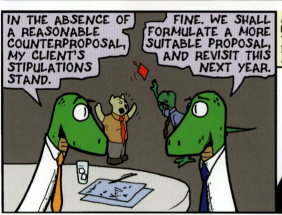

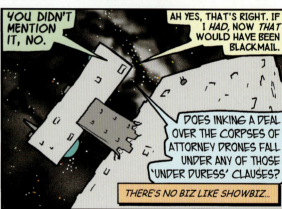

POST POST-DATED-CHECK-LOAN PART I: RAISING CAPITAL OFFENSIVE

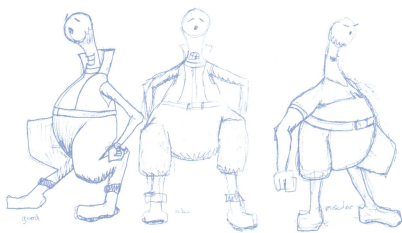

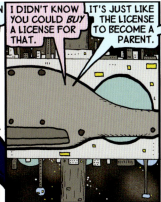

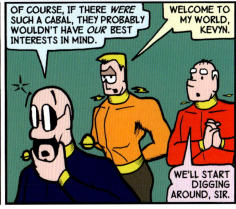

THE TERAPORT WARS

Post Post-Dated Check Loan Part I: Raising Capital Offensive

Note: One of the few sports that remains largely unchanged after an entire millennium is 31st-century baseball. The bats, the balls, the clay, and the spitting are all there. So are the red-faced refs and their shouting matches with equally red-faced coaches.

One improvement is that the process of striking for more pay has become a formalized part of the game. Usually it falls upon the refs to moderate the action, but in a good strike you'll get both teams *and* half the refs sitting down on the field, while the owners and the local political leaders get into the red-faced shouting with the coaches and the union managers.

In a *really* good strike, the extremists in either camp will get called out by their teammates and 'encouraged' to accept whatever compromise is currently leading the real-time fan polls. This encouragement can take many forms, but is typically similar to the encouragement offered to a baseball to get it from just over the plate to a point somewhere left of center.

The fun just never stops at the ball-park. Bring your kids, your lucky glove, and money for some of that sticky biomass they're trying to pass off as caramel kettle-corn.

RJ Price

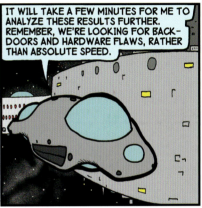

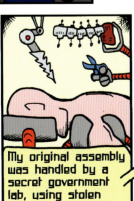

POST POST-DATED CHECK LOAN PART I: RAISING CAPITAL OFFENSIVE

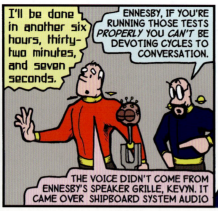

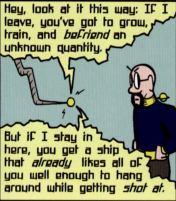

POST POST-DATED-CHECK-LOAN PART I: RAISING CAPITAL OFFENSIVE

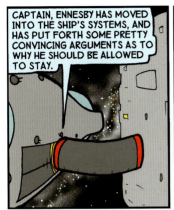

Note: In the waning years of the 20th century a popular self-help book for businessmen, *The Seven Habits Of Highly Effective People*, was lampooned on-stage by an improvisational comedy troupe which only four years later was completely defunct, giving rise to speculation that perhaps those in charge should have been reading the book more carefully rather than lampooning it.

Their sketch, *The Seven Habits Of Highly Effective Pirates*, went completely unnoticed for several centuries, until the day an archeobibliologist named Joel happened across the script in the *Gates Memorial Archive Of Stupid Things From Ye Olde Internet*. Our story would have ended there, except that Joel's younger brother Linc was in prison for privateering, and it occurred to Joel that perhaps his wanna-be pirate brother would get a kick out of reading it.

Unfortunately, Linc realized as he chuckled at the script ("Bury the hatchet! Hah!") that he was in prison because he was NOT an effective person, and was an even less effective pirate. So he began to write.

Most books written in prison do not tend to sell well, but this one did. Eventually, *The Seven Habits of Highly Effective Pirates* was translated from Galstandard West into the other four Galastandard languages (East, Eight, Brown, and Peroxide), and became a handbook not only for pirates, smugglers, and privateers, but also for CEOs, defense attorneys, and tenured professors. The fact that there are more than seven habits, as well as dozens of 'rules,' may confuse some readers, though, so be warned. And remember Rule 12: *A soft answer turneth away wrath. Once wrath is looking the other way, shoot it in the head.*

THE TERAPORT WARS

POST POST-DATED CHECK LOAN PART I: RAISING CAPITAL OFFENSIVE

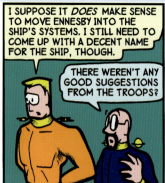

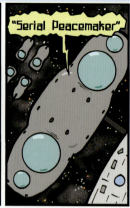

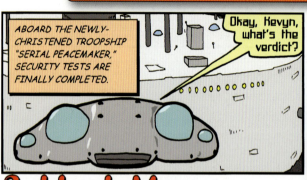

Note: Yes, that's a fiddly-bit on the bouquet. It's either a tracking device installed by the Nefarious Florist's Cartel, or it's there to keep the flowers nice and fresh.

POST POST-DATED CHECK LOAN PART II: TANDEM ACTS OF KINDNESS

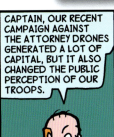

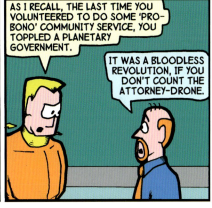

THE TERAPORT WARS — 173

Post Post-Dated Check Loan Part II: Tandem Acts of Kindness

POST POST-DATED CHECK LOAN PART II: TANDEM ACTS OF KINDNESS

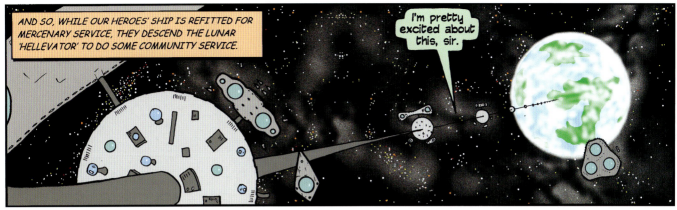

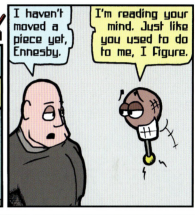

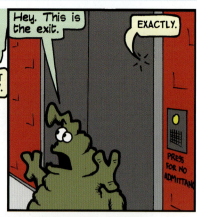

Post Post-Dated Check Loan Part II: Tandem Acts of Kindness

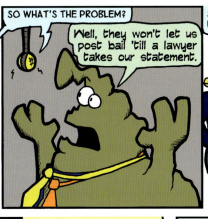

POST POST-DATED CHECK LOAN PART II: TANDEM ACTS OF KINDNESS

Note:
The bounty-hunters employed by Thud Bongo come from varied backgrounds, but most of them have something in common: if they did not work for Bongo, they'd be dead, in high-security prisons, or in the military. In fact all of them have been offered just these options at some point and have wisely (or at least predictably) selected the option that affords them the most personal freedom.

Left to right you are looking at Lex Callister, Carv Dodder, Thud Bongo (whom you've met already), Jevee Ceeta, and Tug Shandal.

All of them are dangerous. None of them are nice. And since their pay and their personal freedom is incumbent upon revoking the personal freedom of others, their non-nicetude varies in direct proportion to their pay.

'Carv Dodder'

THE TERAPORT WARS

Post Post-Dated Check Loan Part III: Handsome Ransom

POST POST-DATED CHECK LOAN PART III: HANDSOME RANSOM

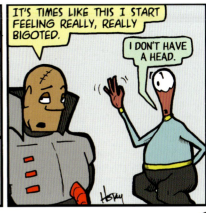

Note: Lex Callister's dialog in the first panel is grammatically incorrect. "Everybody" should have "heads," plural. Lex's error is deliberate. He is attempting to address everybody as individuals, ensuring that each individual's hands go behind his or her own head, rather than somebody else's. It is a bit of finesse completely lost on his audience.

Note: Most Ellies (*elephas maximus sapiens*, the race of sentient Indian elephants) eschew clothing in favor of tatoos, body paints, and earrings. This particular Ellie is a bit odd, however, as evidenced not only by the fact that he chooses to wear clothes, but also by his choice of employment as an air-traffic controller.

THE TERAPORT WARS

Post Post-Dated Check Loan Part III: Handsome Ransom

Artist commentary:

I'm surprised that outside of my own work I've never seen an armored dwarf surfing on a flying axe. You'd think this would become a staple of epic fantasy, what with dwarves crafting such wondrous things, and yet having such short legs.

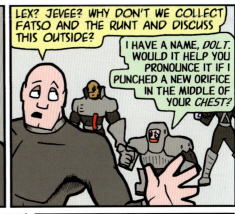

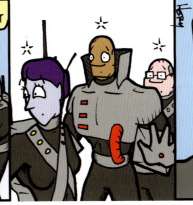

Post Post-Dated Check Loan Part III: Handsome Ransom

Note: When we first met Doyt Gyo and Haban 3122, we learned that his armored suit was 'one-of-a-kind.' The government project that produced him has tooled up to produce at least one more like him: Lex Callister and Haban 1653. Poor Lex still thinks that his Haban lives in the armor rather than in his spine, and Doythaban (whose separate sapiences have yet to completely merge into one personality) is not about to disabuse him of that comfortable illusion.

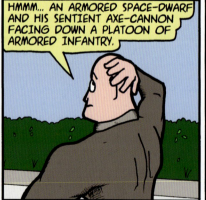

Note: While it's possible that ordinary Doppler radar could be jammed with plain old soup, other, more sophisticated (and more energetic) bands of radar can only be jammed with something significantly less transparent. Not only must we assume that there are iron supplements in the soup, but also that the elephants are showering Tug Shandal with very large quantities of it. While we're at it, we ought to imagine the presence of chunks, gobbets, and other difficult-to-identify meatishly heavy bits, and perhaps some spoons.

POST POST-DATED CHECK LOAN PART III: HANDSOME RANSOM

Note: Haban's reference to "keeping souvenirs" does not apply to his last gig with Thud Bongo, in which he was wrongly accused of keeping bits of the corpse of the doctor he brought in. That accusation stemmed from the fact that in Doyt's early days he DID make a habit of keeping a piece or two of each captured bounty, and it was this reputation that led to the accusations that got him fired (and, by extension, into the current mess).

Don't ask which pieces he liked to keep. Please.

THE TERAPORT WARS

POST POST-DATED CHECK LOAN PART III: HANDSOME RANSOM

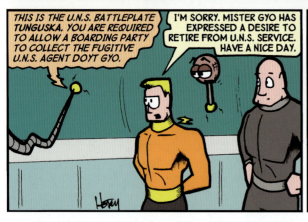

Note: Battleplates were originally designed to protect planets from the sorts of events that create the geographical features for which the Battleplates are named. The student of geology should only need to hear names like "Chicxulub", "Vredefort", and "El'gygytgyn" to know that we're talking about large rocks landing where rocks ought not land.

While it might seem like overkill to have close to a hundred giant ships like these in one planetary system, that's because once you've moved all of the naturally occuring rocks-o'-doom from dangerous orbits, you begin to worry about someone else sending one at your homeworld from an oblique angle, and at velocities more typically associated with charged particles or recklessly-piloted warships.

Should a relativistic rock the size of a house hit your planet, it will ruin your entire day. Battleplates, with their swarms of long-range, hypernetted sensor drones, are insurance against that sort of event. And with their massively overpowered annie-plants, they're good for all kinds of things, including the odd spot of intimidation.

POST POST-DATED CHECK LOAN PART III: HANDSOME RANSOM

Note: Those readers inclined to impart some meaning into the purely subjective similarity between Gaffy and former U.S. President Bill Clinton need to pay closer attention to the details that unmistakeably distinguish the two. Gaffy has actually been *sent* to jail for his indiscretions, and none of them involved cigars.

Note: It was only a matter of time before function caught up with outdated form. Neckties began as handy napkins, and served nicely to keep food from landing on one's shirt. That they proceeded to evolve into something you'd need to use a napkin to protect demonstrates the truth in James P. Hogan's statement: Evolution is not TOWARD something. Evolution is AWAY FROM.

Massey's hypernetted neck-phone is about as far away from being a napkin as it is possible to be, while still being attached to his neck.

THE TERAPORT WARS

POST POST-DATED CHECK LOAN PART III: HANDSOME RANSOM

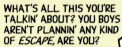

Note: PIGNet is the Perpetrator Identification Galactic Network. The original abbreviation, "PerpID," ended up evolving into "Purple," which caused a small stir among those genetically-enhanced humans with pale violet skin (it's photosynthetic), who felt that using a racial epithet to refer to a database full of information on criminals was inappropriate.

That the name "PIGNet" worked out fine just goes to show that some groups handle being epithet-ificated better than others.

POST POST-DATED CHECK LOAN PART IV: TEMPESTUOUS FUGITIVES

Note: While it has no bearing on the fate of our heroes, Gaffy's story may serve as a handy cautionary tale.

Gaffy followed Schlock, Legs, and Andy out of the cell and out of the jailhouse, at which point he caught a cab and headed home. His wife heard him come in at 0121 local time, and while she was just angry enough to have taken a frying pan to him, she was also sleepy enough to wait until morning when she would be better rested and could swing the pan while it was hot, and full of bacon grease.

Just under three hours later, at 0412 local time, the S.W.A.T. team knocked down the door, stormed the bedroom, and slapped restraints on a very hung-over Gaffy. On their way out the door, Gaffy was struck in the head with a thrown frying pan, at which point his wife was taken into custody on the grounds that she either attempted to assault an armored police officer with a class 2 kitchen implement, or was trying to murder her husband.

The attorney handling her case is also handling her divorce.

THE TERAPORT WARS

POST POST-DATED CHECK LOAN PART IV: TEMPESTUOUS FUGITIVES

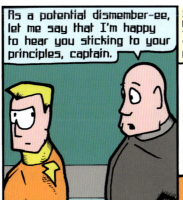

Dave Stanworth
www.snafu-comics.com

THE TERAPORT WARS

Post Post-Dated Check Loan Part IV: Tempestuous Fugitives

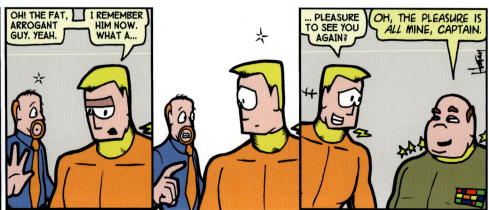

Post Post-Dated Check Loan Part IV: Tempestuous Fugitives

Post Post-Dated Check Loan Part IV: Tempestuous Fugitives

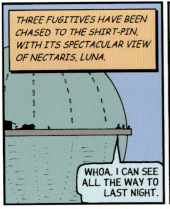

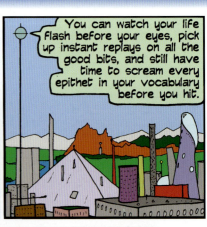

POST POST-DATED CHECK LOAN PART IV: TEMPESTUOUS FUGITIVES

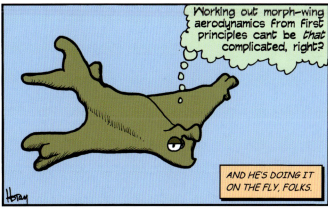

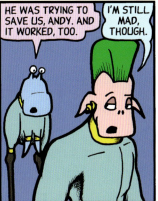

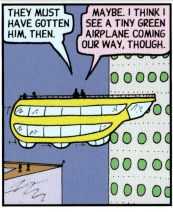

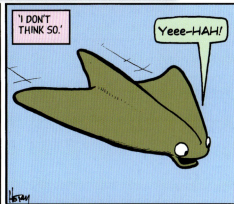

THE TERAPORT WARS

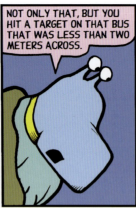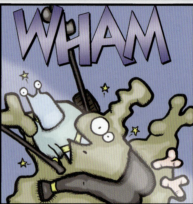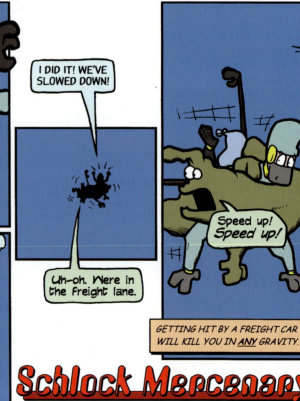

POST POST-DATED CHECK LOAN PART IV: TEMPESTUOUS FUGITIVES

Artist commentary:
Only much later, long after I'd designed him, did I realize that when running like this Andy becomes kind of a centaur pony with pants.

THE TERAPORT WARS

POST POST-DATED CHECK LOAN PART IV: TEMPESTUOUS FUGITIVES

Note: The Nectaris City Police Department was not at all pleased at having to pack all of the mercenaries' gear up and send it back to them. They'd only just figured out what a clean job someone had done refitting Schlock's sawed-off multi-cannons, and were sending someone out for ammunition when word came down to give everything back.

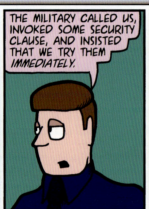

Note: The term "kangaroo court" refers to any impromptu, ill-run, and likely illegal court proceeding. Etymological research indicates that the term found its first use not in Australia (home of the kangaroo, as well as numerous other curious and annoying mammals), but in 19th-century America, in the western territories of the United States.

This fascinating discrepancy has led a few 31st-century anthropologists to suspect a giant U.S. cover-up regarding the extermination and eventual extinction of the Giant California Kangaroo. "Obviously," they say, "whoever did this got a hasty trial."

POST POST-DATED CHECK LOAN PART V: MIGHT MAKES RIGHT OF WAY

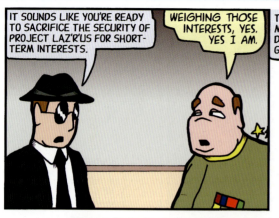

POST POST-DATE CHECK LOAN PART V: MIGHT MAKES RIGHT OF WAY

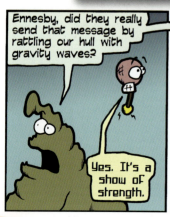

POST POST-DATED CHECK LOAN PART V: MIGHT MAKES RIGHT OF WAY

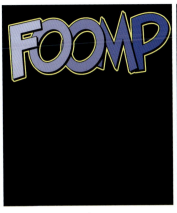

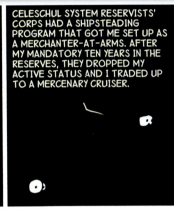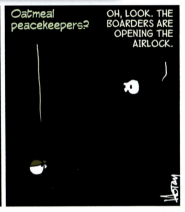

Artist commentary:

I suppose I could comment on the concept art here, but it's much more fun to consider the eye-ball strip above. Ah, yes, I remember drawing that one. Best thirty seconds of my career...

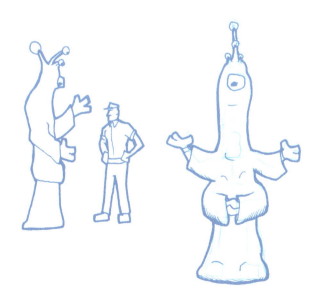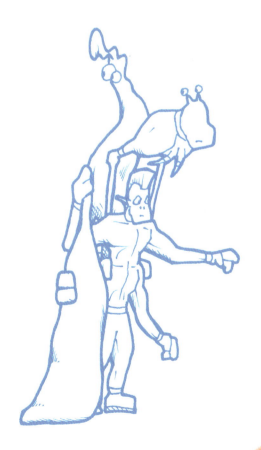

THE TERAPORT WARS

POST POST-DATE CHECK LOAN PART V: MIGHT MAKES RIGHT OF WAY

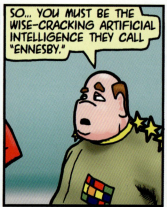

POST POST-DATED CHECK LOAN PART V: MIGHT MAKES RIGHT OF WAY

Note: Plea-bargaining anything *down* to Grand Spamming is usually a bad idea. As early as the 21st century spammers were already less popular than defense attorneys, door-to-door fragrance salesmen, and the French. By the late 31st century they were held in the same regard as pedophiles and telemarketers.

The stigma was so powerful that Hormel was forced to rename their increasingly unpopular luncheon meat to "SPHLEGM" (Salted, Processed Ham and Lard. Edible? Gag a Maggot!)

Sales skyrocketed.

THE TERAPORT WARS

POST POST-DATE CHECK LOAN PART V: MIGHT MAKES RIGHT OF WAY

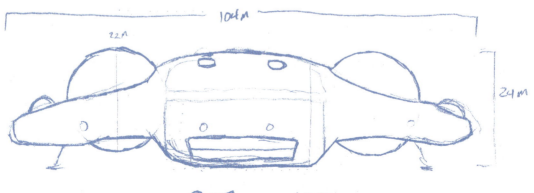

Kevin Wasden
www.splintered-mind.com

Schlock Mercenary
Altered States

Altered States

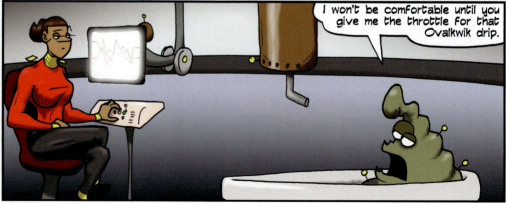

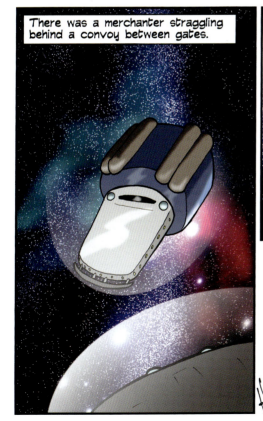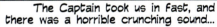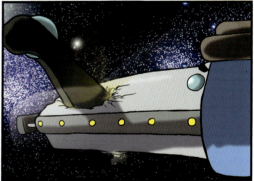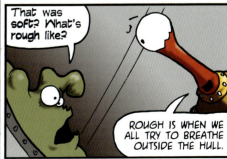

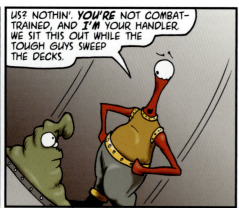

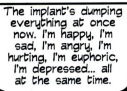

Altered States

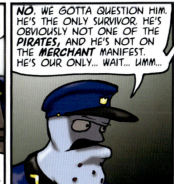

The comic strip pinups seen on p 216 were contributed for use on that page with the permission of the artists. Left to right:

Monica from Wapsi Square, (c) 2001-2008 Paul Taylor, www.wapsisquare.com

Ceciana from Sore Thumbs, (c) and (tm) 2004-2008 by Owen Gieni and Chris Crosby, www.sorethumbs.com

Rayne from BloodRayne, image (c) 2008 Chad Hardin, hardinartstudios.blogspot.com. BloodRayne comics are (c) Digital Webbing, www.digitalwebbing.com

The blue-skinned aliens seen on pp 219-220 and the police sergeant seen on this page were rendered in tribute to my favorite blueskins from Privateer Press. "Trollbloods" are my favorite faction, tougher than nails, and are (c) and (TM) Privateer Press, www.privateerpress.com.

The Teraport Wars

This space intentionally left blank. If there is a picture in this space, it is possible that the author has vandalized your book. It is remotely possible that this was done at your request. Please check your receipt.